STARSTRUCK

A heartwarming, feel-good romance
to fall in love with

EMMA BENNET

JOFFE
BOOKS

Revised edition 2022
Joffe Books, London
www.joffebooks.com

First published in Great Britain in 2020

This paperback edition was first published
in Great Britain in 2022

Cover art by The Brewster Project

ISBN: 978-1-80405-695-0

To my wonderful friend Shirley-Anne. Thank you for all the little, and not so little, things you do for us. Love you.

CHAPTER ONE

Pouring herself a "celebratory" glass of wine, Kate couldn't help her rather melancholy mood. She'd been determined not to feel sorry for herself, but that had lasted no time at all. She wished Charlie were with her. Not knowing when she'd be finished at the solicitors, she'd welcomed her mum's offer to pick her son up from school and have him stay the night. But right this minute, missing his ceaseless chatter and love, the house felt terribly empty, and made the fact she'd just got divorced, and her little family was officially broken apart, even more poignant.

Although only six o'clock, she was hungry and ready for supper. She'd taken to dining early with Charlie since she and Nick had split up; it was no fun cooking just for herself anyway, and she didn't like Charlie eating alone. By now she'd thought he'd have at least one sibling, if not two, but her marriage had hit the rocks soon after Charlie was born. She and Nick had struggled on for the next couple of years, but neither of them had mentioned trying for another child, knowing without having to say the words that their relationship wasn't strong enough to handle it.

Nick had moved out almost two years ago, when they'd both finally had to accept the inevitable. The main thing she'd felt was relief: relief that she no longer had to pretend. Their last years together had been exhausting: the constant bickering arguments had been upsetting, but at least showed some passion lingered; when that withered and died, their rote, coolly polite exchanges masked the indifference of strangers — automatons playing at love, their occasional attempts at affection ringing hollow and false, no matter how genuine the effort. The charade of a relationship, performed to each other, to Charlie and to the world.

Ironically, it was after he'd left that Nick really showed what a good father he could be. He was much more reliable, and far more patient and involved with Charlie, than he'd been when they were a couple. She'd hated to admit it at the time, but they were both happier apart. They respected each other and had even managed to salvage a friendship of sorts for Charlie's sake out of the wreckage of their marriage.

There was no chance of them getting back together, and Kate wouldn't have wanted them to. But today their divorce seemed so absolute. The last nail in the coffin of what they'd had, and the family they'd created.

And so, despite knowing it was for the best and merely the final step of what had been foregone for a long time, for now at least, she was sad.

The telephone's ring broke her gloomy reminiscences and Kate answered it gratefully, "Hello?"

"Hiya lovely, it's me," replied her best friend, Rebecca. Becca was Kate's opposite in looks: tall and curvy with short blond hair and blue eyes, where Kate was brunette, small and slight. Kate didn't see it, but she was very pretty: her delicate features, hazel eyes and thick, tousled, curling locks made an arresting picture.

Kate could hear Becca's two young sons and husband horsing about in the background and it made her heart ache: listening to a happy family going about their evening together was really something she could do without. She focused on her friend's voice.

"I was just calling to check you're alright," Becca continued. "How did today go?"

"It was . . . weird. The whole thing was over so quickly. It seems much easier to get divorced than to get married," Kate quipped, but her friend wasn't taken in by the false cheeriness.

"Do you need me to come over?"

"No, no. I'm fine."

"Kate . . ."

"Okay, I'm not really fine, but I will be."

"Are you sure?"

"Yes, thanks for the offer, but I think I need to be by myself tonight. It's all done now. I can begin to move on properly."

"That's my girl. Let me know if you change your mind though. Call me anytime, you know that."

"Thanks, Becca."

They chatted on for a short while longer, but Kate's hankering for solitude weighed heavily, and the call naturally drew to an end. The house's silent stillness enveloped her suffocatingly, deeper and emptier now in contrast, but speaking to Becca had perked her up a little. It was nice to hear her friend was there if she needed her; she'd known it anyway, but the words were comforting.

Without Charlie around and with no one camping in her field or staying in either of the two barns she rented out to holidaymakers, in theory she could really relax for the first time in goodness only knows how long. But here she was, mooching around, dwelling on the past and feeling sorry for herself. Maybe what she'd said to Becca had been wrong and she should go out, meet up with people — socialise and keep busy, with no room for introspection. But she didn't feel like it. As much as she loathed the solitary atmosphere of her home that night, she needed to be alone.

Kate changed out of the suit she'd worn to the solicitors and into jeans and a sweatshirt, eschewing her favourite cosy top, a relic of Nick's once one-too-many business lunches meant he couldn't fit into it comfortably. She gave her hair a brush and put thick socks on to keep out the chill from her kitchen's flagged stone floor.

There wasn't a lot of choice of what to eat as she hadn't been in the mood to go to the supermarket, but after rummaging through the cupboards, Kate found a big baking potato and popped it in the microwave, grated some cheese and made a bit of a hodgepodge salad from what was left in the fridge. Putting a load of laundry on, more for the comfort of some noise from the machine than any pressing need, she considered laying the table, but dining solo wasn't something Kate thought she'd ever be able to properly get used to. Tired, and a bit emotional, she decided to take her supper for once into the sitting room and have it in front of the television. Funnily enough, something Charlie was never allowed to do.

Kate's home was a small, stone farmhouse, half covered in deep green ivy. Renovating and converting the barns had been the priority when she and Nick moved to Devon, so that's what their money had been spent on — the farmhouse itself, other than a coat of paint or two, had been largely left untouched. Yes, it was a bit old fashioned and needed a touch of work here and there, but it was warm and snug, nothing like the modern interiors of the barns. A family home, filled with toys, books, and usually more than a little bit of mess, it radiated homeliness.

She settled down on the big squishy sofa she and Nick had chosen so the three of them could all snuggle up and put on the television. There was a property programme starting in a few moments and she always enjoyed those. Turning to the right channel, she caught the last part of news. She only half watched it, her distracted mind going over and over the fact she was now officially single again. Her attention was brought properly back to the TV when a photograph of a familiar face came up on the screen. "And finally," read the news presenter in a sombre tone, "The world is in shock after the announcement by rock sensation Joseph Wild and his

4

wife, Golden Globe winning actress Genevieve Moore that they've separated. The pair have asked for privacy for themselves and their five-year-old daughter Ismene." An image of Wild and Genevieve at some award ceremony or other flashed up, followed by footage of Genevieve leaving a gym looking sad, but impossibly beautiful and flawlessly styled.

Kate didn't think about Joseph Wild often, but whenever she saw him on television or yet another magazine cover, she couldn't help but remember the happy times she'd spent with Joe, as she knew him, when they were at school together.

He'd only been at her school briefly: joining at the beginning of sixth form and leaving the following summer in a modern-day fairy tale when his band had landed a huge record deal. His life thereafter, but especially his relationship and then marriage to Hollywood starlet Genevieve Moore, had seemed unbelievably glamorous to Kate. She'd been fascinated by Joe's music career as it took off, and when he fell in love with Genevieve, one of Kate's favourite actresses, he appeared to lead a completely charmed life. But over the years of not being in touch, she supposed she reminisced about him less and less, and while she didn't forget the fun they'd had, her memories didn't seem to fit with the star he'd become.

But she now knew from experience what it was like to go through a divorce, and it wasn't easy, regardless of how rich or famous you were.

She idly revisited the past while the TV carried on with its inane background prattle. Latching on to the pleasant nostalgia, she decided to distract herself with it and set off upstairs purposefully. Where had she put it?

She searched the cupboard on the landing and looked under her bed, concluding a spring clean was definitely long overdue. After an increasingly frustrating quarter of an hour, she finally found it: the scruffy cardboard box labelled "School Stuff" was on top of her wardrobe, under piles of shoes, and a coat of rather dubious taste. Inside was all her A Level work and a pile of photos. Rifling through, she soon spotted a snap of her and Joe: they were sat on the grass in the park just behind the school, laughing at something together, with his arm draped casually around her. The photo brought a smile to her face, along with a barrage of memories.

* * *

Joe hadn't exactly caused much of a stir with the female students when he'd first turned up at school: train track braces, glasses, long hair and his lanky, gangly teenage body, made him more geeky ugly duckling than Proto-Rock God, but he and Kate had become friends straight away. They'd had a couple of subjects together and had got on really well.

They began hanging out after school and Joe fitted right in with Kate and her friends. She knew he was interested in music, it was one of his subjects for A Level, and he spent a lot of time practising. He'd told Kate he played a couple of instruments but hadn't gone into detail: it was just a part of his life outside of their shared activities and friendship.

It was a Friday evening, almost at the end of the school year, when Joe had handed Kate a flyer for a band playing at a local pub the next night, "Come along," he'd said, "The lead singer isn't up to much, but the rest of the group are supposed to be pretty good."

"Okay, maybe I'll see you there," she'd replied, not wanting to commit herself in case none of her other friends fancied coming with her. Joe hadn't suggested they go together, just that he'd be there, so she didn't want to rely on meeting him and have to turn up by herself, especially if she had trouble getting in as she was under eighteen.

As it happened there hadn't been anything else going on the following evening and, finding themselves at a bit of a loose end, Kate's little gang had decided to go and see the band.

The pub wasn't the most salubrious of locations, and the staff certainly weren't bothering to check any IDs, genuine or otherwise, as they took people's money for the performance in the large upstairs function area, complete with its own bar. It had been all new and exciting to her seventeen-year-old self, all very grown up.

Squeezing past the mingling bodies in the darkened room, they made it to the bar. The smell of stale beer thickened the air. She began to surreptitiously scour the throng for Joe, but still hadn't spotted him when the band came onto the stage. They'd launched into their first song and Kate's focus had been immediately drawn to the stage: these guys sounded seriously good. There'd been four of them up there: a drummer, a bass guitarist, a lead guitarist and the singer, who'd also strummed away on a guitar. The singer had begun the lyrics and instantly Kate's attention had been totally focused on him and his strong, gravelly voice. She'd been hooked, taking in every word, and so had the crowd.

It had taken her a few seconds to realise the singer was Joe. He and his group weren't just good, they were amazing! She'd seen her schoolmate in a whole new light, and she'd liked it. He'd looked towards her and somehow, despite the jostling multitude, caught her eye. He'd smiled as he pushed his hair out of the way, and she'd been amazed to find herself blushing. He was just so different on stage; he was, well, sexy!

She'd been brought back down to earth by her friend Claire shrieking into her ear, "Oh my god, it's Joe up there! Did you know he could sing?"

"Nope," she'd shouted back. "I had no idea."

The band had carried on playing, the audience loving them. Their songs were fun and catchy, with a couple of heart-wrenching ballads. But it was Joe himself keeping people enthralled, he'd been mesmerising.

An exhilarated and sweat-soaked Joe had joined them when his band's set finished. "Hey, thanks for coming!" he'd said, kissing her on the cheek. "Did you manage to get that essay done for Miss Blanning?"

"Who cares about a stupid essay Joe?! Why didn't you tell me you could sing? I mean, just wow!"

It was Joe's turn to redden, and all of a sudden he'd been back to being the Joe she knew, her geeky friend. "You liked the band then?"

"You guys were absolutely brilliant."

A big smile had spread across his face, "Thanks!"

A slightly older, muscular guy Kate recognised as the group's bass player had come up and grabbed Joe's arm. "Come on man, there's some record label dude who wants to talk to us. Dave reckons he's the real deal."

"No! Seriously?!" An excited Joe had turned back to Kate, "Sorry, I've got to go; I'll catch you later though?"

"Sure."

But she hadn't seen him later. He'd texted to say he'd been stuck talking to "music people!!!" and hadn't been able to get away until after she'd left. Neither was he around much for the last week of term, certainly not to properly speak to. She'd tried texting him a few times but got no reply. School broke up for summer and the next time she saw her friend was when his band's first single was released and they were featured on *Top of the Pops*. Their lives had moved onto different paths.

* * *

Kate put the photo down and rummaged through the box until she found her notepad from her English A Level. She opened it, and, as she'd remembered, on the inside of the cover was written "Joe". Underneath it was his mobile phone number. He'd scribbled it there at the end of the first class they'd had together. She sat looking at it for a few moments. He wouldn't still have the same number, would he? Should she message him? Self-doubt and uncertainty reared their twin heads. On any other evening that would probably have been it and she would have left the past alone, but her very lack of confidence was itself enough to goad her into action.

Kate took the book downstairs and called the number. It rang several times and she was about to put the handset down, when the answer phone kicked in, a generic message. She heard the beep signalling she should start speaking, and before she could think better of it, said:

"Hi Joe, it's Kate. . . Kate Holloway? You might not remember me; it's been about twelve years, I think! We knew each other at school. Anyway . . . um . . . I was sorry to hear your news and I just wanted to say if there's anything I can do . . . well, let me know. Not that I imagine you'd need my help, but . . . um . . . well, I've just been through a divorce myself so . . . I understand. Bye."

Oh god, why had she come out with that? She was usually eloquent, a good communicator, witty even! So what was that? Now, if he even got the message, he'd think her brain had died over the last decade. She reassured herself it was incredibly unlikely he would ever hear it, he'd probably thrown away that phone years ago — why would he have bothered to port an old number when he'd apparently, as far as she was concerned at least, not kept in touch with anyone from his old life?

A new thought surfaced and joined the queue of embarrassing reflections: were unused numbers recycled . . . Because a random someone may have just been left her incoherent mumblings.

Kate watched the end of her property programme, cleared up and went to bed for a read and an early night, sure that world-famous Joseph Wild would never contact her. She really did doubt he'd have the same number after all these years but was glad in a way that she'd stepped outside of her own problems to try to offer help to someone else.

CHAPTER TWO

The next day was Saturday, and Kate's mother, Susie, brought Charlie back in the morning. Susie was a slightly smaller, more smartly dressed, grey-haired version of her daughter. They were close but independent, with an easy friendship, though Susie was extra protective of Kate since she'd broken up with Nick.

Kate was given a big hug by her mum, whose concerned, questioning gaze she could only answer with a quiet, "I'm ok. I'll give you a call later when Charlie's in bed."

"Alright, but promise me you'll let me know if you need anything. I can stay the night if you want?" Susie suggested.

"Honestly, Mum, you don't need to worry. Charlie and I will be fine."

She gave her mum a reassuring kiss on the cheek; you were never too old to have your mother fret about you she knew. Susie did her best to cheer Kate up, recalling some of her son's antics, before reluctantly leaving.

Kate made sure she kept herself and Charlie busy for the rest of the weekend so she didn't have time to feel down-hearted. It was pretty hard to feel sad with a happy five-year-old around. Then it was Monday, and routine took over. Charlie was back at school and there was plenty of maintenance on the barns and grounds for Kate to be getting on with. Bookings were low as it was only the end of March, so it was a good time to get everything looking perfect for the summer. She was pleased to receive an email confirming a reservation for that night — it was unusual both because it was for a single person, the barns' size and location tended to attract families, and it being a weekday, but she was glad of the business.

Kate was proud of what she'd achieved with the barns. When her Devonshire grandmother died, Kate discovered her family, if not perhaps truly "well off" then certainly "comfortable", had conspired for her to inherit the farm as the only grandchild. She'd been left the barns along with the house and land, though they'd been in a sorry state, the old lady having spent the last years of her life contentedly in a nursing home. She and Nick had sold their little two-bed-roomed terraced house in Tooting, London, and moved to Devon. They'd renovated the barns one at a time, fixing them up together every weekend and almost every evening, both funnelling all their money into the project. It was prob-ably the most at ease they'd been in their marriage: focusing on a common goal, which they hoped would provide them with a very happy, financially sound future. As soon as the first, Apple Barn, was finished they advertised it for holi-day rental. They'd trusted the beautiful rural location would mean it would prove popular, and they weren't disappointed. Within a few months the second, a four-bedroom conversion they named Cherry Barn, was completed, and Kate was able to give up the temporary job she'd found at the local estate agents. Then they began work on the campsite, a large field with shower block, taps and pits for bonfires and barbeques, with a little stream running along one edge and woodland surrounding it.

Ten months later, Charlie was born, and to an outsider, Kate's life was idyllic. But in reality, her marriage was in serious trouble. As Nick's job as a pharmaceutical salesman took him away more and more, Kate was lonely with often only the baby for company. Nick resented Kate, thinking she had it easy, while he was exhausted from a career he didn't enjoy. When he did get home, he seemed to begrudge having Charlie around. He wanted to relax in front of the television with a beer, not sort out bath time and stories for a tired baby. Kate had been with Charlie all day, as well as looking after any guests they had, and would be cooking supper and working her way through the evening routine of a busy home. She didn't think it was too much to ask him to help with his own child.

It got to the point where it was often actually easier when Nick wasn't around. At least then she didn't have to deal with the horrible atmosphere that now seemed to follow him like his own personal bubble of bad temper.

Desperate to keep her family together, despite how bad things were, Kate couldn't bring herself to call time on their marriage. Eventually it was Nick who did. There was nothing momentous about it, no huge explosive fight. It had just been a regular Friday evening. Nick was home late and so had missed seeing Charlie before he'd been put to bed. Kate was determined not to nag or complain though: she'd cooked a nice meal and had hoped they'd be able to spend a relaxed evening together.

They'd been halfway through their spaghetti Bolognese, eating in silence having very quickly run out of things to talk about, when Nick had put down his knife and fork.

"This isn't working," he'd said quietly.

"Sorry?" said Kate, looking up from her food.

"Us. Our marriage, it's not working. I'm not happy."

"Oh," was all Kate could bear to say. She felt the same way, but actually bringing it out into the open was terrifying. Strangely, its surprise introduction as a topic to discuss, like an interesting article from a magazine or sad story from the news, lent it a slightly detached air, robbing it of some of its potentially huge ramifications — which helped. But not much. Butterflies fluttered in her stomach and her mouth turned dry.

Nick put his head in his hands. "I can't carry on like this."

She wondered how long he'd been building up to broaching the subject. And how far he'd thought things through.

"But what about Charlie?"

"This can't be good for him — look at us Kate!"

To be honest, she had to agree. She'd seen the effect she and Nick and their unhappiness were having on their little boy despite their sincerest efforts. Sadly, she supposed it was perhaps time to finally face the inevitable. There was no real going back now anyhow.

"What are we going to do?" she asked quietly.

"I guess that's what we need to work out."

That was the last night Nick spent in their family home. He moved out the following morning.

At first the change seemed unbearable — even with Nick often away, the two of them had been a unit for over eight years, how would she manage by herself, without another adult around to rely on? It wasn't that long though before they'd all got into a routine, and Kate was absolutely certain she and Nick had made the correct decision: being together hadn't been the right thing for Charlie. As peculiar as it was for their little boy to have his daddy living somewhere else, home life was more relaxed without Nick, and when he did see his dad, they had fun together, and his father was more patient with him.

* * *

Kate was hanging up some washing in her garden when she was dragged from her reminiscences by the sound of a car pulling up on the gravel driveway. Using the side gate, she walked round the house and discovered a silver Mercedes, complete with blacked-out windows, parked outside. A figure was standing by her door.

"Hello!" she called. "Can I help you?"

The figure turned round and Kate gave an involuntary gasp: it was Joseph Wild. *The* Joseph Wild. With a guitar and

13

a rather large suitcase next to him. The first thing that flashed through her mind was how funny it was she thought of him as Joseph and not Joe. But the man in front of her was definitely not her geeky friend from sixth form. Naturally, he was still tall, but he was no longer as lanky. His previously dark brown hair was now more of a dirty blonde. It wasn't as long as it had been, but fell across his right eye. She felt an urge to lift it out of the way. Which was probably the very reason his stylist had cut it like that, she contemplated.

Of course she'd seen him on the television many times over the years, and had witnessed his transformation into bona fide superstar, but it was still strange to have him right before her eyes, so familiar, yet so different.

"Kate!" said Joseph, sounding relieved. "It's good to see you, it's been way too long." He walked over and gave her a hug.

This is completely surreal, thought Kate as she stood gawking at her old friend, Friday's crazy phone call replaying cringingly in her mind. Finally she managed to gather herself together enough to ask, "What are you doing here?"

"I'm staying here. Or at least I hope I am," he added swiftly, seeing the look of alarm sweep over Kate's face. "Sorry I'm early; it made sense to slip out of London before the rush hour. My PA made a booking for me last night, under a false name."

"Mr Smith," they said together.

"Exactly," said Joseph, laughing.

"But why here? It's practically in the middle of nowhere!"

Joseph signalled to the driver of the car who started the engine and drove off. He took in Kate's questioning gaze and said, "Um, I've got a bit of a favour to beg of you."

"Okay," she said slowly, "well I guess you'd better come inside then."

Slightly bemused, she led Joseph into her house and through to the old-fashioned kitchen, where she put on the kettle.

"Take a seat," she offered. "Tea?"

"Please. Milk and two sugars."

They waited in awkward silence as the kettle noisily boiled. It was only when she'd presented Joseph with his drink and joined him at the table that she asked, "What's this favour then?"

"I need a place to hide out from the press. They've gone crazy since the news that Genevieve and I broke up hit the headlines. I just need somewhere to lay low for a while and be able to concentrate on work without reporters and cameras everywhere I look."

"But— we haven't seen each other for years."

"You're someone the press doesn't know. And someone I hope I can trust."

"Of course you can, but why me?"

He raised an eyebrow. "The message you left on my old phone."

"Oh," Kate flushed, embarrassed.

"You sounded exactly as I remembered," Joseph said softly. "I appreciate it sounds a bit peculiar, it's just you were the only person I'd heard from who wasn't demanding details. You were checking how I was. Your voice brought back a lot of memories and you genuinely seemed to care about me and weren't after a story like everyone else." He pushed his hair out of his eyes. "My house in LA is surrounded by journalists; I can't go anywhere, do anything, without a camera flashing in my face. I need somewhere quiet and secluded to get my head straight and work out what I'm going to do next."

"Of course but I can't believe you got the voicemail. I think I thought it would just disappear into the ether!"

He laughed. "Well, I've ported the number around. For my mum really. A kind of private line she can always reach me on."

He smiled nervously before continuing, "My PA did a bit of investigating for me. I hope you don't mind. He says you have some holiday homes here and set up the booking. Is it okay for me to rent one? I'm happy to pay whatever you want," he added quickly.

"I've got two converted barns. They're both empty, it's out of season," explained Kate, "You could stay in either of them for as long as you need, but, Joe, how do I know the paparazzi won't descend upon my home? I've got my little boy to think about," she explained.

"They have no idea where I am, my driver managed to give them the slip before we'd even left London, and if they did find out, I'll leave straight away. I promise."

Kate took a moment to consider. It was a really quiet time of year and the money would certainly be handy. As long as Joseph stayed out of the way, there was no reason anyone would know he was here. They hadn't seen one another for so long, it's not like reporters would make any connection between the two of them.

"Yes, you can stay," she said. Joseph let out an exaggerated sigh of relief, making Kate grin.

"Wait a minute! You sent your car away! And you've got your luggage with you! What if I'd said you had to go?"

"I was pretty sure you wouldn't. You can't have changed that much."

"Hmm . . . I'm beginning to suspect you see me as a bit of a pushover."

"Not at all, just a kind person anxious to help out a friend in need," replied Joseph, cheekily.

"I'll get the key to the barn," said Kate. Joseph followed her back into the hallway and she took the keys out of the old oak desk she kept all her paperwork in.

"Is that your son?" he asked, pointing to a photo of Charlie hung on the wall. The little boy was in his school uniform, looking particularly angelic. His usually ruffled light brown hair was neater than usual, and his grin a little self-conscious.

"Yes, his name's Charlie, he's five."

"Same age as my Issy. He looks like you."

"He's got his dad's eyes."

"You said in your message you're divorced. How long?"

"Since last Friday, it's actually what prompted me to call you."

"Oh, that's um . . . recent."

"Yep."

"Are you alright?"

"Getting there," said Kate, "We've been separated a while so . . ." she trailed off uncomfortably. Not wanting to get maudlin, she swiftly filled the expanding pause with an overly-cheerful, "Come on, let's get you settled in."

As they walked along the tree-lined track leading to the smaller barn, Kate took the opportunity to properly assess her old friend. His clothes were clearly expensive; she wasn't taken in by the artfully distressed look. In fact, he wouldn't have looked out of place in an MTV music video with his carefully messed up hair and biker boots. She did notice though that he still had the same ever so slightly cautious walk, not the confident swagger she associated with "celebrities" used to strutting down red carpets at any opportunity.

He caught her watching him and smiled. "Have I changed?"

"In some ways, not so much in others," said Kate with a laugh.

"Well, you haven't!"

Kate pulled a face and he added, "Not much anyway."

"I like your hair longer," he said, taking a strand of it gently in his hand.

Kate felt a surprising shiver run through her at his touch. She looked up and their eyes locked.

"What happened to your glasses?" Kate asked in an effort to defuse whatever was happening.

"Laser eye surgery."

"Right," she replied, turning away.

Get a grip, she told herself. How pathetic, going all gooey over a rock star. What was she? Fifteen? She was a grown woman! A mother! Anyway, he was married! He and his wife had only just split up, it was perfectly plausible they could get back together once they'd calmed down from whatever argument they had. They were probably both temperamental, being showbiz types and had overreacted to a little disagreement of

17

some kind . . . This was simply her old friend Joe coming to stay for a while. That was all. There was no need for any awkwardness, and surely she could manage some poise and dignity.

They reached the stone barn with its oak door and potted olive trees either side of the entrance. Crossing the threshold, Kate felt a little tingle of panic that it wouldn't be good enough for her A-List guest. She thought the holiday homes were great, and had put a lot of effort into making them lovely, but he'd be used to luxurious five-star hotels, not the rather more homely service she prided herself on providing.

She'd taken him to the smaller of the two barns as it would be just him staying, but now she wondered if she'd made the right decision. Was the other barn nicer? Would he have preferred more space? Would he expect to be given the biggest accommodation available as he was such a VIP?

All of a sudden nothing seemed like it could possibly be good enough; never before had she looked at her business through such critical eyes. Surely there were a million places far more suitable for him to hide out in? She really should have suggested somewhere else.

The downstairs of both barns had a Scandinavian feel, with a soft blue and white colour scheme and pale wooden floors throughout. The front door opened straight into the double height sitting room area, complete with a pitched ceiling and skylight. The bedrooms and main bathroom were over the kitchen and dining areas. The other house had a study type room downstairs, as well as an extra bedroom with an en suite. Maybe the office space would have been handy if he had business he needed to do while he was here . . .

Joseph followed her inside, looking around. Kate was going to ask if he'd like to see the other barn in case he preferred it, but before she could he'd kicked off his boots and flopped down on one of the two large sofas facing the open fireplace, proclaiming, "This is perfect, thank you."

"Are you sure it's alright? I mean, I know it's probably a bit basic compared to what you're used to . . . there's no . . . hot tub or anything," Kate explained hastily.

"I don't need a hot tub!" laughed Joseph, "Honestly, it's great. I can really feel your influence on the place. You've done a fantastic job."

"Oh! Thank you. Um . . . is there anything you need? I usually put a few bits in the kitchen, milk and teabags, that sort of thing; I'll bring them round later."

"Thanks, that would be great."

With a shy smile, Kate left.

* * *

Charlie was dropped off at five by Kate's mum who'd taken him to his swimming lesson after school. Susie was in a rush so Kate didn't have a chance to explain the events of the past few hours. Not that she was quite sure just what she would say. It wasn't that she didn't trust her mum not to give away anything, but she'd said she'd keep Joseph's visit a secret and wouldn't feel comfortable breaking his confidence, however much she was dying to talk to someone about it!

She gave Charlie a bath and helped him into his pyjamas.

"Let's get tea sorted out, shall we? What would you like?"

"Pizza please, Mummy!"

"No problem, little man. You do some colouring while I cook."

Kate prepared the dough and left it to rise while she made a tomato sauce. She was peeling an onion when there was a knock at the door. Drying her hands, she went to answer. It was Joseph.

"Hey," he said, "I don't suppose you have a menu for a takeaway that'll deliver here?"

"I'm afraid none of them deliver, you'd have to go and pick it up."

"Ah. Country living, eh?"

She smiled. "Yep."

"Thanks anyway," he turned to go.

"Would you like to have dinner with Charlie and me?" she asked before she could change her mind. "It's only pizza, but I can easily make enough for you."

19

"That's very kind, but I wouldn't want to impose on your family mealtime." Joseph's hopeful tone didn't quite match his words.

"Honestly, it's no trouble. I can't have you starving while you're staying here. Anyway, it'll give us a chance to catch up properly," Kate said, flushing slightly.

"Okay, thanks. I'd like that."

He followed her through to the kitchen where Charlie was still happily colouring.

"This is my son, Charlie. Charlie, this is Joseph, an old friend of mine."

"Hello, Joseph," the child said, looking up.

"Call me Joe. That's what your mum used to call me when we were at school together."

"Were you Mummy's boyfriend at school?" asked Charlie, staring at Joe intently.

"No, I wasn't."

"Why not?"

"Because she was far too good for me," Joe replied, giving Kate a wink. Kate concentrated fiercely on the onion she was chopping.

"Can you help me?" Charlie asked Joe. "There's too much sky, and my arm's so tired."

"Sure," said Joe, sitting down beside Charlie and accepting the offered blue crayon.

Kate watched them out of the corner of her eye as she cooked. Both seemed to be taking their work very seriously. They muttered to each other now and again, but she couldn't make out what they were saying.

"Food's ready guys, can you clear the table?"

Charlie put away his things and showed Joe where the cutlery was kept as Kate served up.

"I hope this is alright," she said, putting Joe's meal in front of him.

"It looks wonderful. Pizza is my absolute favourite," said Joe, tucking in.

"Mine too!" said Charlie cheerfully, "Mummy, when we're finished, can Joe come up to see my room?"

"Um, yes, of course, as long as he doesn't have to rush off?" Kate said, turning to Joe.

"Absolutely nothing to rush off for. I'd love to see your room, Charlie."

"And read me my story?" asked the little boy hopefully.

"Charlie . . ." began Kate.

"That would be fun, if it's alright with your mum?" Joe said.

"Sure."

They finished eating and Kate sent Charlie to brush his teeth.

"Can I help with the washing up?" asked Joe.

"It's fine, I don't think you'll manage to get Charlie to wait any longer before he gets to show you his room anyway," Kate replied with a laugh, indicating the little boy who'd returned and was practically hopping up and down with excitement in the doorway.

Joe and Charlie disappeared upstairs. Kate could hear her son's voice chattering away and dull thumps as he presumably showed his new friend absolutely every toy he owned. Eventually things quietened down, and if she listened really carefully, she could make out the rumble of Joe's deep voice as he read to Charlie.

Kate washed and dried the dishes, put on a load of washing, swept the floor and wiped down the old pine table and the sides, but still Joe didn't come back down. With time getting on, she decided she'd better check everything was alright.

She went upstairs and poked her head around Charlie's bedroom door. Joe was still reading aloud, but quietly; Charlie, surrounded with teddies, was fast asleep next to him.

"Hi," Kate whispered.

"What do you think? Is he out for the count?" said Joe, getting up gingerly so he didn't disturb the sleeping child.

"I reckon so." Kate gave Charlie a kiss and covered him with his duvet then pulled his dinosaur curtains closed. He let out a happy sigh.

"Would you like a cup of tea?" she asked as they tiptoed back downstairs.

"Well, yeah. That would be lovely. Unless you'd rather get rid of me?"

"Not at all, it's nice to have some company after Charlie's in bed for a change." She put on the kettle. "How much did you read him? You were up there for ages."

"He said you always read him ten stories. He was counting meticulously."

"The little fibber! I'm so sorry! He usually gets three. He obviously thought you were a soft touch."

Joe laughed. "Don't worry, I didn't mind. It was nice. He's a great kid."

"You're very good with him."

"I've been missing reading stories to my daughter, Issy. It's our thing that she bargains with me for how many she can have."

"Where is she now?"

"With her mother," Joe replied shortly.

"Oh." Kate thought it best to drop the subject as he didn't seem to want to talk about it.

Joe wandered over to the window and looked out over what could be seen of Kate's wilderness of a back garden, its overhanging trees and overgrown flower beds vague in the twilight.

"Big garden," he commented.

"Yes, it is." She grasped onto the subject, trying to restart the lost easy flow of conversation. "It needs a lot of work though. But there never seems to be the time, and I can't afford to get anyone in to do it for me at the moment. That out-of-control leylandii in the corner has to come down before it falls down, and I'm desperate to make a vegetable patch by the green house. And clear some space for chickens by the south wall."

"That sounds amazing. It's a great place you've got here," he said, accepting his drink from Kate.

"My grandmother left the land and the main house to me when she died. The old barns were in a pretty bad state, but we renovated them and set up the camping field."

"It's very peaceful."

"Yeah, it's quiet now, but we're very popular once it gets a bit warmer. It's good to be able to run the business from home and be around for Charlie. I don't need to worry about having to take time off work if he's ill and can't go into school."

"And your mum's nearby?"

"Yes," Kate said smiling. "She moved to a little cottage just a couple of miles away when Nick and I broke up. She was very sweet — she'd just retired and wanted to downsize and move out of London, but mainly I think she was worried about me being by myself and wanted to help out with Charlie. She's been absolutely brilliant."

They went into the sitting room and continued the business of filling each other in on their many years apart and news of their families. The longer Kate spent in Joe's company, the more she began to unwind and see him as just a regular guy. He certainly didn't act like a famous star as he sat on her sofa, sipping tea from a Transformers mug.

Eventually she stifled a yawn; it was past eleven. She'd been up early and the long day was catching up with her.

"Sorry," she said.

"Don't be. I'll get out of your hair and let you relax. I'm a bit of a night owl and now's the time I work best. I ought to see if I can find some inspiration for one of the new songs I'm supposed to be writing," said Joe, standing up and putting on his jacket. "Have a good night." He kissed her on the cheek, sending a tingle down her spine, "And thank you."

Kate's brain jolted back into action again, and she found herself saying, "Oh, hang on a minute; I'll give you the stuff I mentioned earlier, some teabags and things to keep you going."

She hurried into the kitchen, grabbed a carrier bag and tried to think what Joe might need. She had a cupboard set aside for supplies for the barns, but it wasn't particularly well-stocked at the moment. She grabbed a packet of teabags, a jar of coffee, sugar and some biscuits. She found an unopened pint of milk in the fridge along with some eggs and butter, and wrapped up half a loaf of bread. At least he'd have enough to make himself a hot drink and something for breakfast.

She ran back out and handed the bag to Joe, "Here you go!" Her self-consciousness flooded back and she felt almost painful embarrassment at giving him an old supermarket carrier bag stuffed with oddments.

He peeked inside. "Excellent, thank you."

"It's really no problem. I do it for all the guests . . . normally I'd have gone shopping for some locally produced stuff and would've put it in your kitchen for you before you arrived, but you were early," Kate rambled, a little worried Joe would think she was giving him special treatment. "Take a light with you, it's dark," she added quickly and handed him the torch she kept by the front door.

"Thanks, I'll drop it back tomorrow."

Kate stood and watched his fading silhouette as he walked to the barn, her thoughts completely muddled.

CHAPTER THREE

Kate walked Charlie the mile and a half along the hedge-rowed country roads to school the next morning, as she liked to when the weather was mild enough. It was a gorgeous day, the first almost warm one of the year, and it was lovely to feel the sun, weak though it was, on her face. It was good to amble along with her son, listening to his ramblings and pointing out their favourite things to one another along the way. She came back home to pick up the car and the list of errands she needed to run. Scanning over what she'd written, it occurred to her that Joe would need some food, unless he was going to survive on the few bits she'd given him the night before — he couldn't just slip into the town for a pint of milk. She decided to go over there and check if he wanted her to get him anything while she was out.

Catching a glance of herself in the hall mirror, Kate stopped to tidy her wind tousled hair. It could probably do with a wash actually, she considered, but she hadn't had a chance during her super quick shower earlier. Should she do it now before going to see Joe? But then she'd either have to go over to see him with soaking wet hair or waste more time blow-drying it — something she never usually bothered to do.

And what about what she was wearing . . . The jeans and hooded sweatshirt she had on were fine for what she had planned for the day, but she doubted it was the sort of outfit the women surrounding Joe typically wore. He'd probably think she was a terrible slob, she decided, eyeing her reflection judgmentally.

Kate was about to go upstairs to change when she stopped herself. She was being ridiculous. She looked perfectly fine. The same as she'd looked perfectly fine when she'd hung out with Joe the day before. She'd never go to any special effort when she was simply meeting up with friends, why should seeing Joe be any different?

A voice inside her head stubbornly pointed out that this was different; he was a friend but he was also extremely good-looking, charming and world renowned. Kate chose to ignore it and marched out of her front door in the direction of Joe's barn.

Though Kate had been up for hours, she worried it would be a bit early to disturb him. She spotted he'd opened the kitchen window, so figured he must be out of bed at least, but was glad when Joe saw her as she approached the house and came to the door to greet her.

"Good morning," she said, "Did you sleep okay?"

"Like a log," he replied, smiling.

"I was half expecting you to be up all night. I've heard what you rock star types are like."

"I gave up after a couple of hours, no inspiration was forthcoming and I was pretty tired by then. My few truly rock and roll nights are well and truly behind me."

Kate laughed. "I'm off to the supermarket later. I thought you might need some stuff picked up, seeing as you can't really go down to the local Tesco when you're trying to stay incognito."

"That'd be great. Would you mind if I wrote down a few things?"

"Not at all, I've got errands to run and I'm meeting some friends for lunch so I'll be going in about half an hour."

"Excellent, I'll drop my list round in a bit," said Joe, with a smile which made Kate feel like her insides were melting.

* * *

A while later Kate heard a knock at her front door. "Come in!" she called.

"It's just me," Joe said, holding up a scrap of paper. "Here you go. Shall I give you some money for what you're picking up now?"

"Nah — we'll just sort it out when I get back."

"Thanks again."

"It's no trouble. I'll slip round this afternoon after I've collected Charlie from school. Will you be in for the rest of the day? If not, I can let myself in and pop the food away for you if you want?"

"I'll be in; I've nowhere important to go. And I forgot to pack my fake beard for sightseeing," he said smiling. "Seriously though, thanks for doing this for me; I hope I'm not being too much of an inconvenience. Usually I'd get someone to pick up this sort of thing, but I gave my staff a well-deserved break. They've been working like crazy recently and it didn't seem fair to drag them to the UK with me when all I'm doing is hiding out. Most of them have stayed in the States. It's only my driver who's in the country. He's on standby in case I need him, but I'd feel mean getting him to drive here just to get me some groceries."

"That's very good of you, and you're not an inconvenience at all."

He shrugged. "They've put up with a lot the last week or so, and they've all been very loyal. And I'm not completely selfless: it's nice to have some space just to myself. I can be as grumpy as I like without worrying about offending anyone!"

"Sounds pretty good to me. Right, I have to get going or I'll miss my friends. I'll see you later."

* * *

Kate usually liked spending a day pottering around in the car, getting a few jobs done and having lunch out, yet today she was actually quite anxious to get back home. She'd enjoyed Joe's company the night before and wanted to see him again. She knew he said he was fine being by himself, and she understood that, but his current situation couldn't be easy for him and it was nice to have the option of companionship if he changed his mind.

Subconsciously she hurried everything, including her monthly get-together with some of the other mums from Charlie's class in La Casa, her favourite Italian bistro, and ended up arriving at the school gates more than a quarter of an hour early to pick up Charlie. She didn't have time to go home and come back, so waited in the car, looking around at the mess — mud-covered wellies in the footwell, toys, discarded bags, a picnic rug — and vowing for the thousandth time to thoroughly clean it . . . soon.

The stereo was on, and a song from Joe's last album started to play. She turned it up. She knew a lot of his songs from hearing them on the television and the radio, but hadn't bought any of his albums since the first one he'd released with his band. She wasn't sure why: she hadn't deliberately not purchased them, but she'd been hurt by what she'd considered to be Joe's dumping of her as his friend as soon as he got his record contract. She knew he must have been busy, and probably overwhelmed, dealing with loads of exciting new experiences and learning about how the music business worked. She supposed he and his band mates had been completely reinvented as a marketable "product", but even so he could have called, texted or emailed once in a while, even if it wasn't possible for him to actually meet up with her anymore.

And she hadn't been the only person to miss Joe. His own mum had never seemed to know exactly where in the world her son was, let alone when he'd be back to visit. She and Kate had bumped into each other every now and again while Kate was still in the sixth form, and Kate would always ask about Joe and let his mum know that she'd love him to get back in touch. She was thrilled for him when his band's first album was released and became something of a minor celebrity at school herself, thanks to her association with him. But this soon faded when it became clear that Kate didn't see him anymore and knew as much about his new life as anyone else. When she went away to university the following year, she lost the little contact she had with his mum and the only updates she had about Joe came from the interviews with him that she soon gave up reading.

That was all a long time ago, Kate reminded herself. They were both different people now, adults. And could she honestly say she wouldn't have acted the same way towards Joe if it had been she who'd become rich and famous, instead of going on to lead a pretty ordinary, if pretty happy, life?

* * *

Finally, she drove a rather talkative Charlie home. The little boy had hurried inside and Kate was just beginning to unload all the shopping from the car when Joe ambled down the track from the barn.

"Hey, you don't need to lug my stuff around for me, I can get it!" he called out cheerfully.

Kate couldn't help the grin spreading across her face at the sight of him, "You do realise what a truly bizarre mixture of food you've chosen? I'm not quite sure how you plan to make proper meals out of beer, Marmite, crumpets and Branston Pickle, but it definitely won't constitute a balanced diet."

"Hmm, you could be right there! It's been a while since I've shopped for myself, I guess it shows."

"It looks like you missed at least a few things about the UK!"

"I've missed a lot," Joe replied, catching her eye. He opened his mouth to say more, but Charlie's face appeared in the doorway. He was still wearing his school uniform, though it didn't appear quite as neat as when he'd left the house that morning. "Hi, Joe! Look at my dinosaur picture," he said enthusiastically waving a piece of paper.

"That is completely awesome," Joe said, turning to give Charlie his full attention and studying it carefully.

"Will you play football with me?" Charlie asked him pleadingly.

"Charlie, sweetheart, Joe might have work to do," said Kate.

"I haven't actually. I haven't been able to write anything new for months — I've been strumming away trying to come up with some inspiration for hours today, but no joy."

"That must be frustrating."

"It is, but it means I've got all the time in the world to play football with you, Charlie." He grinned at the little boy before glancing back at Kate. "If it's alright with your mum?"

"Of course it is," Kate said.

"Hooray!" exclaimed Charlie excitedly.

"If you'll give me a hand putting away my shopping first," said Joe.

"Sure! I'm really good at putting away shopping."

"Just don't put him in charge of anything breakable. And check the freezer compartment carefully afterwards," warned Kate, quietly.

Joe gave her a wink before focusing back on Charlie.

"You know, I've got a little girl who's about your age. Her name's Issy, and she's crazy about football."

"Can she come and play as well?" asked Charlie.

"Not today I'm afraid."

"Why not?"

"Well, she's with her mum at the moment."

"Can she come and play another day?"

"I hope so," said Joe, following the little boy outside. Charlie was using both hands to carry the lightest bag, its bottom alternating between being dragged along the gravel and being soundly kicked into the air by well-meaning small feet.

Kate sighed to herself as she watched the pair walking and chatting together: why did kids always have to ask such tough questions?

* * *

A short while later and Charlie came running in to grab his football.

"Love you, Mum!" he bellowed, hurrying straight out of the back door into the overgrown garden where Kate could see Joe waiting for him.

Kate finished putting away her own shopping and got Charlie's after school biscuit and drink ready.

"Would you like a cuppa?" she called out to Joe.

"Yes please!" he said, turning to answer her as Charlie sent the ball whizzing past him.

"Goal!" shouted the little boy excitedly, doing a victory lap of the lawn.

"Come in for your snack Charlie," said Kate laughing.

They both traipsed into the kitchen grinning.

"A custard cream for you too?" Kate asked Joe.

"Of course."

"What would you like for tea, Charlie? Pasta or sausages?"

The young boy looked serious for a moment, debating this knotty conundrum, then consulted a higher authority, "What do you think, Joe?"

"It's a big decision, mate. I think you should find out what would be with the sausages before you commit yourself."

"Mum, what would be with the sausages?"

"Mash, carrots, peas and gravy."

"Sounds pretty good to me," said Joe sagely.

"Sausages, please," agreed Charlie.

"Would you like to stay and eat with us, Joe?" asked Kate.

"Oh yeah, please stay," begged Charlie.

"I'd love to." Then, to Kate, he said, "Why don't I bring over a couple of the beers you picked up for me to go with it?"

"Great."

Joe and Charlie went back into the garden to get a little more football in before it got dark and Kate made a start on dinner.

A feeling of contentment washed over her as she pottered about the kitchen and listened to the happy babble drifting in through the open window. The early evening air cooled her as she cooked, and the delicious smell of the sausages frying made her stomach rumble in anticipation.

The telephone rang and she answered it, "Hello?"

"Hi lovely, it's me," said Becca's voice. "Just checking in to see you're alright. I've missed you at the school gate the last couple of days and we didn't get a chance to speak properly at lunch earlier with everyone else there. How are you? Have you seen Nick since the divorce was finalised?"

"I'm fine, thank you. Nick hasn't been round, he's got Charlie this weekend though, so I'll see him then," answered Kate lightly, wishing she could tell her friend about her super famous guest. It wasn't that she couldn't trust Becca, she was sure she could, but she'd promised Joe she wouldn't tell anyone and she wouldn't break that promise. "What about you?"

"Work's been a bit of a nightmare, but when isn't it? Other than that, everything's good."

Joe and Charlie chose that moment to thunder into the kitchen, Charlie on Joe's shoulders, singing "We Are the Champions" at the top of their voices.

Joe stopped when he saw Kate was on the phone, "Sorry," he mouthed, and took Charlie, who was still singing, out of the room.

"What on earth was that?" asked Becca, laughing. "Why is there a man singing in your house?"

Kate frantically considered what she should say. She was a terrible liar so sticking as close to the truth as possible was probably sensible. "He's an old acquaintance. He's been playing football with Charlie."

"What 'old acquaintance'?" said Becca, immediately picking up that she wasn't being told the whole story. "Is he staying with you? You dark horse!"

Panicking as she didn't have any answers prepared for this sort of inquisition, Kate quickly said, "Oh yikes!" drowning out Becca's disbelieving laughter. "Sorry, I've got to go, my potatoes are boiling over! I'll speak to you properly soon,"

Once she was off the phone, Kate went to find Joe and Charlie.

"Sorry about disturbing your call," Joe said immediately.

"Not to worry, it was only Becca, a friend of mine; I think she found it rather amusing."

Joe's questioning look led her to say, "Charlie sweetheart, go and wash your hands, you've been playing outside." When the little boy had left the room she said, "Don't worry, I didn't tell her."

"Thanks."

"Although, I probably do need to come up with a proper explanation. I just said you were an old friend playing football with Charlie."

"Well, that's okay, isn't it?"

"What if Charlie says something at school?"

"It'll be fine. He calls me Joe for a start, not Joseph Wild. He doesn't know who I am and it's not like anyone would suspect you're harbouring a mega talented rock god."

"Mega talented? Really?"

"A direct quote, thank you, from *Music Hits* magazine."

"Did you or your agent pay them to write that?"

"Neither." He laughed. "But thank you for doing a fantastic job of keeping me down to earth."

"It's a pleasure."

Kate tried to bring them back to the problem at hand, "But if I say you're here to play football, won't people find it a bit strange when you're still here days later?"

"You have pretty nosy friends."

"Seriously!"

He shrugged. "Just say I'm an old school chum staying for a while."

"*A single man coming to stay with a single woman*? They'll think we're together. If you're here when they call, they wouldn't know you're actually renting one of the barns."

"So?"

"Well, maybe I don't want people to think I've moved a lover into the home I share with my son the week after my divorce!"

"I think you're overanalysing this, Kate. Other people have got their own lives to lead. They're not going to be that interested in the fact you've got someone staying, unless they thought it was Joseph Wild, and they have no reason to think that."

She sighed. "You could be right. I don't like the idea of lying to my friends though."

"You're not lying to them; you're just not telling them my full name and occupation. But I don't want to make life difficult for you or make you feel uncomfortable. I can leave any time, just give me the word," Joe said, soberly.

"No, I don't want you to leave," said Kate immediately. "You're right, I'm overthinking things."

Charlie came back into the room and bounced straight over to his new best friend.

"Right, Charlie," said Kate, "You can watch some cartoons until food's ready. This 'mega talented rock god' here is going to peel some carrots for me."

CHAPTER FOUR

Kate was in the middle of some washing up a few days later, when the phone rang, heralding another awkward conversation.

Charlie was playing with his Lego in the sitting room so she called through, "Can you get it please, Charlie?"

"Okay, Mum!" he replied, running in and picked up the receiver. "Hello? . . . Oh hello, Grandma! . . . I'm fine . . . I played hide and seek with Joe and now I'm making a space ship."

Kate took off her rubber gloves and motioned to him to pass her the phone before he could go into any more detail about what he'd been doing with Joe, but he was so engrossed in his conversation, he didn't see her gestures.

"No, Joe's not at school, Grandma!" he said, giggling. "He's Mum's friend. He's staying here. He's really fun and good at football."

Finally, Charlie noticed his mother's frantic arm movements. He looked confused for a moment, but then it clicked what she wanted.

"I think Mum needs to speak to you," he said, and passed the telephone over before wandering off into the other room to resume his building.

"Hiya, how are you?" said Kate chirpily, hoping to swiftly change the topic of conversation to her mother's arthritic knees or the evil neighbourhood cat who kept digging up her freshly planted gladioli.

"I'm fine dear, but who's this 'Joe' Charlie's talking about? Have you got a boyfriend?" she asked hopefully, before, rather contrarily adding, "I don't mean to pry, but isn't it perhaps a bit early for a man to be moving in with you, I mean you can't have been together very long."

"Joe's not living with us, Mum, don't panic," Kate replied, inwardly cringing at having to explain her actions to her mother, who'd leapt to the exact conclusion she'd known everyone would. "He's staying in one of the barns. He's just an old friend from sixth form," she expanded, and then could have kicked herself as she realised she'd given away far too much information.

"I don't remember you having a school friend called Joe," Susie said, pausing thoughtfully, "Except that lovely boy who went off to become terribly famous. I wonder how his mother is. Now, what was his surname? I saw him on the telly quite recently . . ."

"Wild, Mum."

"Oh yes. Did you know his marriage has broken up? He was married to that gorgeous actress Genevieve Moore, and they've got a beautiful little girl. Same age as Charlie. Anyway, it seems no one knows where he is, probably hiding out somewhere . . ."

Susie went silent as she worked out the implications of what she'd said. Then she whispered, as if afraid the phone might be bugged, "You have Joseph Wild staying in your barn, don't you?"

"Yes," admitted Kate eventually. "But you mustn't tell anyone! I promised him I wouldn't say anything and if the papers find out he's here, it'll be dreadful for Charlie and me. Charlie would be terrified having journalists camped outside, shouting at him every time we try to leave the house."

"Of course I won't say a word. The man should have some privacy if that's what he wants. And you didn't tell me, I guessed. But how exactly did he end up in your barn? I thought you hadn't spoken to him for years."

"I hadn't. It's bizarre really: I . . . well . . . I kind of left a message on his old mobile number when I heard he and Genevieve had broken up. It was the same day my divorce came through. I guess I didn't think he'd actually ever hear it! But then he just turned up on my doorstep wanting to stay!"

"He's been here with you for more than a week and you haven't said anything to me!"

"I couldn't, I'd promised Joe!"

"I'm sure he didn't mean you couldn't tell your own mother," came the indignant response.

"And I'm sure he did."

"Well, you just be careful."

"I will, Mum."

"Shall I pop round to pick Charlie up from school for you tomorrow? Save you doing it?"

"Are you only saying that because you're hoping to catch a glimpse of Joe?" asked Kate, laughing.

"No!" replied Susie, a little too quickly. "Can't a grandmother just want to spend time with her grandson without having an ulterior motive?"

"Of course, Charlie would love you to pick him up," said Kate, making a mental note to ensure Joe was well out of the way before her mum's visit.

"See you tomorrow then. Say good night to Charlie from me. Oh, and to Joe of course."

"Joe won't be coming round tonight," Kate said, but her mother had already ended the call.

* * *

Kate felt a little nervous as she got off the phone. How would Joe react when she told him her mother knew about him staying with her? She'd faithfully promised not to tell anyone, and she'd meant to keep that promise — it was important to her, important that Joe trust her. She'd been so stupid to slip up like that. She should have been more cautious with what she'd said. Then again, with her mum living close by, and often coming to help look after Charlie, it was almost inevitable she'd find out about Joe. And Kate could hardly lie to her if she asked why someone was staying for such a long time in one of her barns. Maybe she'd been wrong to let Joe stay at all. She had a life to lead, and Charlie to care for. She shouldn't be wasting her time hiding rock stars needing a bit of a break from their enviable lives.

Yet Kate knew she'd never have been able to turn down Joe's request for help. Not once she'd seen him. He'd only been back a very short time, but he already seemed to have fitted perfectly into her life, filling a gap she'd been aware was there, but hadn't known how to deal with. She had no idea how long he'd be around for, or what the future held for them. Would he abandon her again as soon as he left, the way he had all those years ago? Or would they keep in touch?

She could hardly imagine her and Charlie jetting off to LA to visit Joe, but stranger things have happened. What was so frustrating was there was no way for her to know whether they'd still be in contact in only a week's time! He could call his driver in the middle of the night and simply vanish out of her world — she wouldn't even have the means to speak to him again unless he chose to contact her. What was there keeping him here? Nothing really, apart from any attachment he felt for her and Charlie.

Kate had to tell Joe her mum knew Joseph Wild was staying in her barn, but she wasn't looking forward to doing it. What if he decided to leave as soon as he heard what had happened? He didn't know her mother well at all; he'd only met her a handful of times, years ago. He might decide that choosing to trust her to keep his secret was just too much of a risk to take.

Still, there was nothing for it; she had to be honest with him, regardless of the consequences.

Luckily she didn't have long to wait as Joe turned up just a quarter of an hour later. Charlie was in his bedroom so she had the perfect opportunity to speak to Joe without little ears around. She steeled herself as he poured them both a drink from a newly opened bottle of Pinot Noir.

"Joe," she began, "I've got something to tell you."

"This sounds ominous," he replied.

"I'm so, so sorry but my mum knows about you being here."

Joe's face fell as he processed the ramifications of what she'd said. Kate quickly continued, "It wasn't intentional: Charlie said too much and I tried to cover it over, but I ended up giving the game away — I'm sorry, I'm just useless at lying. Though I think it was inevitable she'd find out. Mum and I are pretty close; you know she's around a lot helping me with Charlie."

Joe was quiet for a moment. "Will she tell anyone?" he asked eventually.

"No. I explained what might happen if she did; the media circus we'd have here. She adores Charlie. She'd never subject him to that."

"I can't imagine she would," agreed Joe. "But if you're worried, I'll leave straight away. I promised you I would when I first arrived here, and I meant it."

"I don't want you to go, and I really don't think there's any need for you to," said Kate, hurriedly.

"Good. I don't want to either," he admitted.

"So does that mean you're planning to stay for some time?" Kate asked, turning away and busying herself at the sink to assume an air of false casualness.

"As long as that's not a problem . . ." Joe replied. "If you have someone else booked in . . ."

"No, no. As I said, there's no one booked in to your barn. I just wanted to know."

"Well, I'm hoping you'll be stuck with me for a while longer."

"That suits me," said Kate, hiding a silly, irrational, schoolgirl-crush thrill of excitement behind a smile, "Can you give Charlie a call for me, please? I'm just about ready to serve up."

* * *

On Friday Kate hadn't long returned from picking Charlie up from school when Joe knocked on the front door.

"I'm not interrupting anything, am I?" he asked.

"No, of course not, come in," said Kate, attempting to smile.

"Charlie left his football with me yesterday and I thought I'd better return it."

"Ah, thanks."

Joe looked concerned. "Are you okay? You seem sad."

"Yeah, I'm fine, only Charlie's going to stay his dad this weekend. It's the first time since the divorce was finalised and I'm feeling a bit . . . maudlin, that's all. I still haven't got used to him not being around when he's with Nick."

"Ah, I see."

"I know it's silly. He just makes so much noise; it's too quiet without him here. And because it's the weekend, all my friends have plans with their own families, so it's not even like I can meet up with them and distract myself."

"Well, I'm free. Why don't we hang out?"

She gave him a look. "You're an internationally famous celebrity, you must have better things to do than hang out with me, even when you're in hiding!"

"Nope, I really don't." He grinned. "This weekend I am dedicating myself solely to cheering you up."

"And how exactly do you plan to do that?"

"I'm a little unsure of the specifics, but the general idea will be to keep you so busy, you won't have time to miss Charlie."

Kate gave him a sceptical look. "Well, not as much as usual anyway," Joe amended. "When's he off to his dad's?"

"Tomorrow morning, Nick's picking him up at nine."

"I'd better get going then; I've got some adventures to prepare. I'll see you tomorrow at nine thirty. Is it alright if I go and say goodbye to Charlie?"

She nodded, warm feelings of gratitude and affection mixing with the general undercurrent of sadness, "Of course you can. And Joe? Thanks."

"Not a problem, it'll be my pleasure."

* * *

When Kate went to put Charlie to bed later, her heart melted when he threw his arms around her and pulled her tight to his body.

"Hey little man, that was lovely. What did I do to deserve such a fab cuddle?"

"Joe said you might need an extra big snuggle tonight."

"Thank you, sweetie. I did."

"Joe's nice, isn't he?"

"Yes, he is."

"I hope he stays for a really long time."

"So do I," replied Kate quietly.

CHAPTER FIVE

Charlie was in a questioning mood over breakfast the next morning.

"How long is Joe going to be staying here?" he asked, munching on his Rice Krispies and interrupting her humming along to Kylie on the radio. Kate suspected he'd been thinking about their conversation from the night before.

"I don't know, sweetheart," replied Kate lightly, though the exact same thought had been going round and round her own head, despite Joe's assurance that he wouldn't be leaving anytime soon.

"Is he on holiday?" continued the little boy.

"Well, sort of."

"Because we always know how long we're going away for when we go on holiday."

"Yes, we do. Would you like some Marmite on your toast?" Kate asked, hoping to distract him.

"Yes please, Mum. Will Joe go to live with his little girl?"

"I hope so, he must miss her very much," said Kate carefully.

"He must," agreed Charlie thoughtfully. "I don't live with my daddy either do I?"

"But you see him lots though, don't you?"

"Yeah. I hope Joe gets to see his little girl soon."

"Me too," Kate replied, giving him a hug. She couldn't imagine being apart from Charlie for even as long as Joe had been apart from his daughter already, let alone not knowing when she would see her child again. It would crush her to have him as far away as Issy was from Joe. He still wasn't keen to talk about Genevieve, but Kate knew he was missing Issy terribly and he spoke about her more and more often. It made it worse that he was having such a lot of trouble getting through to Issy on the phone — Genevieve was reluctant to take his calls and, if she deigned to, was obstructive in putting him through to his daughter.

She just wished there was some way to help Joe, but how?

* * *

Although it was awkward seeing Nick for the first time since the completion of their divorce, Kate found handing Charlie over the smallest of fractions easier than usual knowing she had her mystery adventure to look forward to.

True to his word, Joe was on her doorstep at nine thirty on the dot.

"Good morning!" he said cheerfully.

"Good morning, Joe," Kate replied, smiling.

"Are you ready for the fun to begin?"

She laughed. "As ready as I'll ever be!"

"Right well, as I'm technically in hiding like some bizarre guitar playing fugitive from justice, our fun will have to be of the rather undercover sort, but I haven't let that deter me, oh no."

"So what are we going to do?"

"We're going to the seaside."

There was a pause before Kate commented, "Won't that be a little chilly, and, you know, likely to have people about?"

"It will be a bit nippy, but definitely not crowded. This beach is private and owned by a friend of mine. It's ours for the day, along with his boat."

"His boat?"

"Yep. Bet you didn't know I could sail, did you?"

"No, I did not!"

"You'll need a complete change of clothes, and you might want to swap that top for something warmer and add a couple more layers, but everything else will be there for us. Can we take your car? I could send for mine, but it tends to attract attention."

"That's fine," said Kate with a laugh, excitement bubbling and spirits lifting at the thought of the day ahead. This was an awful lot of trouble to go to to cheer up a friend; she couldn't help wondering, could it be possible that Joe was after something more?

* * *

Luck was most definitely on their side as far as the weather was concerned. The sun actually had some warmth to it and they both needed sunglasses, though Kate called Joe a prima donna when he pulled his out of his jacket pocket as soon as they got in the car.

Kate kept her Renault Clio to the back roads where she could enjoy the beautiful scenery of the area, rather than risk being caught in a traffic jam, staring at the back end of a smelly lorry for the journey. She loved watching the greenery zip by as she tore down the open roads.

"Which bay are we going to?" Kate asked as signs for the coast began to appear.

"Just follow my directions, and stop being so nosy!" was Joe's reply.

Soon afterwards he indicated to a narrow farm track coming up on their left. "Turn down there," Joe instructed.

The rutted dirt way became a more formal driveway, and eventually, they arrived at a huge, white, art-deco style house.

"Park anywhere: no one's in apart from one or two of the household staff," Joe explained.

"Are you sure your friend doesn't mind us being here?" Kate asked anxiously.

"Not at all, we're pretty close."

Kate stopped the car and they got out. She breathed in the crisp sea air, tasting its tangy freshness. The house stood alone atop a small cliff, gulls wheeling noisily high above its roof, their cries joining the faint melody of the breaking waves far below. Joe pointed out a trail which ambled down to a small sandy cove.

"Wait here, I just need to pop inside for a moment," he said. He was jogging over to the house before Kate could ask if there was anything she could do to help.

He pushed the door open without knocking, and went in. Kate felt a slight sense of awkwardness being alone on a stranger's property, but Joe returned a moment later with a large rucksack slung on his back.

"And you're sure your friend is fine with this?" Kate checked again.

"Absolutely," Joe replied. "Come on."

They wandered down the path. The beach was sheltered by two high craggy headlands. A jetty jutted out into the sea to their left with a fully rigged sailboat tied to the end, bobbing cheerfully up and down on the waves.

Even as shielded as they were, there was a steady breeze which whipped Kate's hair around her head.

"Put these on," Joe said, handing her a baseball cap, bright red cagoule, and a life jacket.

"Very fetching," Kate muttered.

"Stop complaining. Look we'll match," he said, pulling an identical life jacket from the bag.

"That doesn't make it better."

"You'll be grateful for it when we're on the water, believe me." He moved towards her. "You need to do it up right to the top," he said pulling the zip up fully. Their eyes met and held. Kate's knees gave more than just a little wobble. Joe seemed to hesitate for a moment, uncertainly etched on his face, then said cheerfully, "Come on, let's get on the water," and the moment passed.

They walked onto the wooden jetty.

"It's not a very big boat, is it?" Kate said apprehensively, scrutinising the dinghy.

"That's the general idea. It's a racer. It's called a 'Fireball'. They've been using the design for over fifty years, but they're a bit faster than they were." He laughed.

"Wait, you race?"

"Yep."

"Are you any good?"

"Nope!"

"But you're, you know, like safe to drive this thing?" asked Kate nervously.

"*Sail.* You sail a sailboat. And yes, I'm quite safe, just not fast enough to win any trophies."

He stepped confidently onboard and held out his hand to help Kate. She hesitated.

"Hey, you can trust me," Joe said. "You know I'd never do anything to put you in any sort of danger."

Kate nodded and got on the boat. It lurched to one side, wobbling alarmingly and she let out a squeal.

Joe smiled, but quickly tried to hide his amusement. "Sit down over there," he said. "It'll balance the boat out. And hook your feet under that," indicating one of two long wide straps running either side of the cockpit.

Kate did as she was instructed and watched as Joe deftly hoisted, unfurled and generally busied himself about various nautical activities until the two white sails filled with a "whumph", and they were underway. Joe talked her through everything he was doing as he made fine adjustments to their heading and sail trim, all the while bobbing up and down, leaning precariously it seemed over the side to keep the 'heel' of the boat right. None of what he explained really went in, but it was reassuring that he clearly did know what he was doing.

The bracing wind meant they kept up a good speed.

"How far are we going?" Kate asked.

"Not far. We'll just work our way around the headlands and bays. Are you ready to give sailing this boat a try?"

"Yes," said Kate resolutely.

"Then shuffle over here and take the helm."

A couple of exhilarating hours of hard work later, and Kate felt she at least knew what needed to be done to keep the fast little boat gliding over the sea, even if actually doing the manoeuvres was clumsy at best. Most importantly, she hadn't fallen overboard or made a complete fool of herself in front of Joe.

They anchored in a sheltered cove for lunch and Joe produced thick, doorstep white bread sandwiches filled with honey roast ham and mustard. They washed them down with hot, strong coffee from the flask also stowed in the rucksack.

"Your friend made you lunch and left it for you to pick up?" Kate asked incredulously.

"Well, his housekeeper did."

They set sail again after their break and Joe attempted to teach her how to beat to windward. It had never occurred to her before that you couldn't just sail a sailboat directly into the wind. They alternated between helm and crew, for no matter how hard she tried, they made no forward progress, just tacked back and forth, when she had the tiller. She couldn't help but admire Joe's very evident skill and found it rather . . . distracting.

"How did you learn all this stuff?" she asked at one point.

"When the band first went over to the US, our manager had some boats at the Florida Keys and showed me the basics. I've done quite a bit over the years, with cruising yachts and racing catamarans and dinghies like this."

"I do remember seeing photos of you on boats in the paper; I thought you were only posing!"

Joe pretended to be affronted, "Not at all! I'm a regular sea dog me."

He checked his watch, "We'd better head back if we don't want to be working against the tide. And the wind's meant to be picking up."

Kate executed her smartest gybe of the day, without slipping over this time, and with a few instructions from Joe, soon had them making good headway towards home. She was inordinately proud when she managed to bring the boat to a stop almost right alongside the jetty. Another thing she'd never thought about until today was how did you stop a sailboat? It has no brakes or even an engine to put in reverse.

Once they were on dry land, Kate quickly began to feel cold. She'd been working surprisingly hard sailing and as she cooled down she realised how wet she was. Particularly once the ghastly-looking life jacket and soaking wet cagoule were off her and the wind cut through her damp clothing.

Noticing her shiver, Joe made her race him to the car to warm up again.

"Grab your spare clothes from the boot," he called back, beating her easily. "You can get changed inside. The downstairs cloakroom is the second door on the left," he said as he let himself into the house. "I'll put the kettle on and refill the flask."

Kate got her clothes and went inside. It felt peculiar to be entering someone else's home without them there, but Joe was obviously sure it was alright. She found the cloakroom, which was so pristinely white she worried about dirtying it with her mucky stuff, and quickly changed. She immediately felt much warmer and set about attempting to tidy her rather windswept hair, but soon gave it up as a bad job. She cleaned up the now mud-streaked floor as best as she could with water and some toilet paper, thinking wryly that she couldn't be taken anywhere nice.

Coming back out into the large entrance hall, Kate wasn't sure what direction the kitchen was in.

Listening intently, she could make out noises coming from towards the back of the house and decided to follow them. She opened a door into a huge, modern kitchen. There was a large island in the centre surrounded by stools. Light flooded in from French doors on one side of the room, through which lay an incredible view of the bay which Kate found hard to pull herself away from. Everything was bright and gleaming. Joe stood by the stainless-steel fridge, its door open.

"Are you really stealing food from your mate's fridge?" Kate asked making him jump.

"I'm not stealing! He'll be fine with it. It's only a bit of chicken — want some?"

Kate raised an amused eyebrow.

"Suit yourself. I've made us tea. Shall we take it out into the garden as the sun's come out again?"

"That sounds like a great idea," said Kate.

They drank their tea on an old cast iron bench at the bottom of the long lawned garden, watching the sun getting lower in the sky, and talking until they began to get cold again and took the mugs back inside before getting in the car and beginning the drive home.

They were just approaching the main road when they passed a large, familiar looking silver Mercedes going in the opposite direction, to the house they'd left.

"That's weird," commented Kate.

"What?"

"That car looks just like the one that dropped you off at my house, when you first arrived."

"Surely there must be a lot of cars that look like that," Joe replied, looking unconcerned.

"I guess . . ."

Dusk was falling when Kate pulled up on her driveway.

"I've had a brilliant day, thank you so much, Joe," she said, climbing out of the car.

"Not a problem, it's been a lot of fun for me too. But," he paused mysteriously, "it's not quite over yet."

"No?"

"You have an hour to relax and get ready and then you're expected at the barn in your fanciest frock for a very swanky dinner at seven thirty."

She laughed. "Yes, sir!" And saluted happily.

Kate raced inside and up the stairs excitedly. She couldn't remember the last time she'd got properly dressed up for dinner.

She ran herself a hot, deep bath, pouring in a huge dollop of the Jo Malone nectarine blossom and honey bath oil she'd treated herself to over a year ago, and had been saving for a special occasion ever since. She lowered herself slowly into the water, letting it soothe her tired muscles and feeling her body relax.

She dragged herself out of the tub when her skin was thoroughly wrinkled, dried herself and blow-dried her hair.

She rifled through her wardrobe, knowing exactly what she was searching for, and just hoping it was as lovely as she remembered. There it was. Her vintage 1950s cocktail dress — sleeveless, cream with red printed poppies and flared out from the waist. She put it on and immediately felt transformed into Audrey Hepburn in a scene from *Roman Holiday*.

She found some cute red kitten heels she'd forgotten she even had but decided not to wear them until she was downstairs: Kate hadn't worn any type of heel for so long she'd probably have an accident before she even got to dinner.

* * *

It was properly dark as she walked along the flagstone path to what she now subconsciously referred to as "Joe's barn". The moon was full, but she still needed a torch to light her way.

Trees obscured the view of the building from her house and so it came as a surprise to see a car parked outside, it must have come down the separate track leading behind her garden to the barns from the road without having to go past her own house. Were others joining them for supper? She felt a wave of disappointment: she'd assumed it would just be the two of them, someone else eating with them would feel like an intrusion. She'd thought she'd read the signals right during their day together and had assumed Joe would also want to be alone with her. She supposed she was consciously not analysing it as the idea scared her a little: he was a famous star, it's not like anything between them could really go anywhere. And aside from that, he was technically still married. But she was fed up with always thinking things through, always doing the sensible thing. For once she'd decided to just throw caution to the wind, to go with the flow and her emotions, and see what happened.

It seemed that either fate, or Joe himself, had other ideas though. Maybe it was for the best? There was no point in trying to deny to herself the fact that she was very attracted to Joe, and knew she was liable to get very hurt.

As she got closer, she could see at least two figures moving around in the kitchen and a horrible thought flashed into her mind: what if she'd got completely the wrong end of the stick and Joe had invited a date? That would be excruciatingly embarrassing! It would be obvious she'd gone to some trouble, he'd never seen her so dressed up before, and he'd know it was for him! Whoever he'd invited would be ridiculously beautiful and glamorous. Probably another film star like Genevieve, or maybe some incredibly cool lead singer of a band. But what could she do? It's not like she had time to quickly rustle up her own date now, and she couldn't not go. Not only would that be rude, but it wouldn't be very hard for Joe to walk to her house and find out why she hadn't come!

She contemplated turning round and rushing home to change into something less dressy, something that mightn't look like she'd put in far more effort than it now seemed the evening warranted. But it would no doubt take her ages to decide what to wear, and anyway, Joe had asked her to dress up. Plus, if she had to face Joe's date, she may as well do it looking her best, she resolved. With a deep breath, she marched onwards.

She knocked on the door and it was opened a moment later by Joe dressed in a dinner suit. He smelt of expensive cologne and looked as if he were off to some major music award. This was definitely not the Joe she knew as a teenager, or even the guy who'd been hanging around her house recently. This was an extremely sexy, sophisticated man, and Kate felt a nervous flutter in the pit of her stomach.

"Hey you," said Joe, smiling. He leant in to kiss her on the cheek and the flutter went up another notch. "You look amazing."

"You're only saying that because it's such a shock to see me not wearing jeans," replied Kate.

"No, it's because you look amazing."

Kate blushed, she wanted to answer, but found she didn't have the faintest idea what to say.

"Come on in," said Joe softly, stepping aside and seeming to sense her discomfort.

Once she wasn't quite so close to Joe, a delicious waft of whatever he was cooking hit her.

"Something smells great, what have you made?" she asked.

Joe looked a little sheepish, "I may have had a little help with the cooking," he admitted.

"A little help?"

"As in, I hired a chef. And a waitress."

Seeing her incredulous look, he added, "I wouldn't possibly have had time to cook and get all togged up!"

"I thought I was being treated to your cooking!"

"Now, that's not my fault. I was very careful not to claim I was doing my own cooking. My cooking is awful. I merely invited you for supper here."

"Hmm, very tricksy!"

"Trust me; what Jean-Claude has prepared is a million times better than the burnt cheese on toast you would have endured if I'd been in charge."

"Jean-Claude?"

"He's a chef at my favourite restaurant La Maison, in London. He's technically on paternity leave, his girlfriend had a baby a couple of weeks ago, but they happened to be visiting her family who lives vaguely near here, and he agreed to help me out tonight."

"Does anyone ever turn you down for anything?"

"Of course they do!" said Joe, pretending to be affronted.

"When?"

"I don't have an actual example at hand, but they do. All the time."

"Sure . . ." said Kate laughing.

"Come on through and meet Jean-Claude."

Joe showed her into the kitchen, which looked busy but incredibly organised. There were various interesting-looking contraptions on the worktops that Kate knew didn't come from the appliances supplied with the house. Jean-Claude must have brought a fair amount of gear with him.

The chef himself was by the stove where he divided his attention between three pans. He turned as they came in.

"Jean-Claude, this is Kate. Kate, Jean-Claude."

"*Bonsoir*," replied Jean-Claude lightly, taking her hand and kissing the back of it. The chef was extremely handsome with his long, dark hair and intense eyes. He was very tall and Kate was sure he knew just the effect his looks and strong French accent could have.

"That's enough of that thank you, Jean-Claude," said Joe.

"Do not worry my friend, you know I only have eyes for one woman. You are safe."

"You're incorrigible," Joe replied, laughing.

"Congratulations on the birth of your baby," said Kate, changing the subject, but secretly pleased by Joe's reaction.

"Thank you," Jean-Claude grinned. "She is beautiful like her mama, and likes to be up all night like her papa."

Kate peered over to look in the pans. "It all looks wonderful," she commented.

"It will be," Jean-Claude said confidently.

"I'm afraid I haven't had a lot of say as to what we're actually eating," Joe said.

"You should just be grateful I have come to cook for you," came the chef's retort.

"It's not like there's not some sort of financial gain in it for you," Joe replied. "Rather a large financial gain actually," he added.

"And my food will be worth every penny."

"Now that I'm sure of," replied Joe. Turning to Kate, he said, "Come and see the dining room," and led her out of the kitchen.

Kate was greeted by a smiley young woman who had just finished putting the finishing touches to the pristinely laid table, complete with candelabra. "Good evening, may I get you a drink?" she asked.

"Yes please, that would be great," replied Kate as Joe said, "Lovely."

"Champagne?"

"Wonderful," Kate said, raising her eyebrows at Joe as the waitress poured two glasses.

"I wanted to thank you a little for everything you've done for me. You've really gone out of your way when you didn't have to. I mean, you haven't seen me for years, and you have your own life to lead."

"What are old friends for, even friends who haven't seen each other for a very long time?"

Joe and Kate were handed their champagne and clinked flutes.

"You know you really didn't need to go to all this trouble," Kate said, taking in how beautifully the table had been set — fancy, solid silver, cutlery had even been brought in to replace the rather utilitarian stainless-steel stuff she provided in the barn's kitchen.

"Don't you like it?"

"Yes, of course, everything looks amazing. I just want you to know, I would have been happy with the cheese on toast. It's your company I was looking forward to."

"It won't be my company you'll be thinking about once you taste Jean-Claude's cooking."

"He's that good?"

"Yep."

The waitress returned with smoked salmon canapés, so light they seemed to melt in Kate's mouth almost as soon as she bit into them. They moved into the sitting room and talked food: Joe was quite the gourmet and had eaten in some amazing restaurants over the years.

"I can't believe how many places you've been! You've travelled all around the world," Kate commented.

"I have, but to be honest, I haven't necessarily seen that much of it! When I'm touring it's often just airports and hotel rooms I spend my time in. I try to get out and do some sight-seeing when I can, but the schedule is usually exhausting."

The first course was ready, white wine was poured and tiger prawns dripping in garlic butter were served. The main course of venison with a red wine jus followed and then crème brulée for pudding. "Now this I made sure Jean-Claude put on the menu," said Joe, cracking the crunchy sugar top. "His crème brulée is the best I've ever tasted."

Kate couldn't help but vigorously agree as she tucked in herself.

* * *

Coffee and delicate hand-made truffles were produced and Jean-Claude packed up his gear and the waitress wiped down the kitchen.

"This has been a wonderful day, Joe," said Kate, sipping her espresso, "Thank you so much for organising it all."

"My pleasure, it's been fun. And really good to be able to get out for a few hours."

The alcohol she'd drunk made Kate more candid than she'd usually be and she blurted out, "I do worry though that with you being used to all this amazing food and visiting so many places, spending an evening with me and Charlie, eating boring old pasta and garlic bread, must seem quite a let-down."

"I'd rather spend an evening with you and Charlie in your home than go to any fancy restaurant. I love your cook-ing: it's delicious. It's what I look forward to after a long day. Jean-Claude's food is fantastic, but you couldn't eat it all the time," he said quietly, exaggeratingly checking over his shoulder to ensure their chef was nowhere near.

Kate giggled.

"I've loved spending time with you again," Joe said, holding her gaze. "It's made me remember how much fun we used to have together, just messing around and chatting."

"Until you deserted me to become rich and famous," pointed out Kate.

"Yes," Joe answered, shamefaced. "I did desert you, and I'm sorry."

"I was only joking!" said Kate quickly. "You had the opportunity of a lifetime! Your dream came true; of course you had to seize it. I wouldn't have expected you to turn it down just so you could continue to hang around with me. Never in a million years."

"No, but I should have kept in touch."

"Well . . ."

"It all happened so fast. I know it's a cliché, but my life literally changed overnight, and it took a lot of adjusting to. I was hardly in the UK at all after the first few months. By the time the initial excitement was over, and I'd come back down to earth and realised how much I missed my old friends, I'd left it too long and didn't feel I could call you. It also seemed a bit ridiculous to complain about how hard I had it. I wouldn't have blamed you for putting the phone down on me."

"I would never have put the phone down on you. You should have called."

"I know. I never stopped thinking about you though."

They sat in silence for a moment, contemplating the past, and how different things could have been until Jean-Claude came over to let them know he was ready to go.

* * *

Jean-Claude and the waitress left, with Joe promising to bring Kate to the restaurant once Jean-Claude was back working there.

"It's been an absolutely wonderful day," Kate said again, collecting her things together and perhaps delaying leaving, just a little. "Thank you so much."

"Do you have to go?" Joe asked hesitatingly.

"Did you want to watch a film or something?" Kate replied, as lightly as she could manage.

"That's not . . . quite what I had in mind," Joe replied, moving towards her cautiously, gauging her reaction. It may have been a while, but Kate's body clearly knew what it wanted to do, and she let herself sink into Joe's arms and then into the deep kiss that followed. She looked into his eyes and saw there her old school friend, someone she trusted, but also really, really fancied. When she kissed him, it wasn't some world-famous rock star she was with, it was just a guy who made her feel all tingly and happy, and had gone out of his way to make her day very special. It felt right that this should be the ending of that wonderful day, and the continuation of the relationship between them that they'd rebuilt over the last few days. Of course this was what they should be doing, why in the world hadn't they got round to it sooner?

CHAPTER SIX

It took Kate a few moments to adjust when she awoke the next morning, and to remember why she wasn't in her own bed and didn't have any clothes on. She felt Joe move. He turned and draped an arm over her, pulling her closer. The events of the previous night came flooding back and she smiled sleepily. She felt happy; warm inside. It had been a long time since she'd woken up with a man, but she was certain she'd never felt this level of euphoria on any other "morning after".

She crept out of bed and into the hallway, making her way to the bathroom. She went in and locked the door. Standing by the sink, Kate gazed at herself in the mirror, pushing her tangled hair off her face and screwing up her nose at her reflection. There hadn't been any opportunity to take off her make-up the night before, and her eyeliner and mascara had smudged, giving her panda eyes.

Kate's mood abruptly changed: what was she doing? Women like her didn't sleep with men like Joe. How could she be seducing an internationally famous rock star? Joe was used to being with Genevieve Moore. She couldn't ever compete with that she thought, taking in every one of her tiny imperfections. She never usually worried about this sort of thing, and actively tried not to compare herself to others, but in this case it was extremely hard not to.

She wondered whether Joe had only slept with her because she was all that was available but, then, she had to admit that wasn't what it had felt like at the time. And there'd been the waitress last night who he could have got together with, if all he'd wanted was someone to share his bed. He hadn't had to end up with Kate.

Kate pulled herself up to her full height of five feet, three inches, and told herself to stop being so ridiculous: she was spoiling what had been a magical night. If Joe hadn't wanted to sleep with her, he wouldn't have. It was as simple as that. And the man in the bed now was most definitely her friend Joe, not Joseph Wild. Neither she nor Joe had made any promises for the future which could potentially be broken, but they had a few more hours together before reality, in the form of Charlie, returned late that afternoon, so she should stop wasting time worrying and enjoy herself. Kate ran her fingers through her hair, gave her reflection her best movie star smile, and returned to her lover.

* * *

They took advantage of having no plans or responsibilities for the day and stayed in bed until lunchtime when hunger drove them up. Showering together took away thoughts of food temporarily, but afterwards, when they realised there really wasn't much to eat in the barn's kitchen, they walked over to Kate's house where she made scrambled eggs on toast.

It began to rain heavily, so it was a natural choice for them to cuddle up on the sofa together with a film. After some good-natured bickering, they settled on *Casino Royale*, plenty of action for Joe, and plenty of Daniel Craig for Kate, she teased.

They chatted throughout, more interested in one another than the story on screen, and simply comfortable in each other's company with their easy rapport.

When the film finished, it was almost time for Charlie to return. Kate sent Joe back to the barn so he wouldn't be spotted by Nick; she didn't want to be answering any awkward questions from her ex. Joe was only just out of sight when Nick's car pulled up outside the house. Kate came outside to welcome Charlie and wasn't surprised when Nick came over. He occasionally joined her for a cup of tea when dropping Charlie back so they could chat about their little boy or make arrangements for the next time he'd be staying with his dad.

"Hiya darling, did you have a good time?" asked Kate when Charlie ran to her for a welcome home hug.

"Yeah! It was brilliant! We went to the park and made pancakes!"

"That sounds great," Kate laughed. "Cuppa?" she suggested to Nick. She'd much rather he left so Joe could come back over and join them again, but she didn't want to be unfriendly, and he might have something he wanted to discuss with her.

"Sure," replied Nick, giving her a hello kiss on the cheek.

"Would you like a drink, Charlie?" called out Kate to her son who was rapidly making his way up the stairs to his bedroom and his much-missed toys.

"No thanks, Mum!" he hollered back happily.

Nick followed Kate into the kitchen and took a seat at the table. "You're looking very well," he commented as she got down the mugs.

"Thank you."

"Anything to do with this Joe guy I've been hearing so much about?" He appeared to be attempting a certain level of nonchalance but was failing miserably as he fiddled with a coaster and avoided Kate's gaze. Delicate subtlety was not one of his talents.

Kate didn't answer straight away; she was trying to come up with a suitable response. She knew Nick had been on a few dates since they'd separated, but there hadn't been anyone serious, and certainly no girlfriends had been introduced to Charlie. Joe was an old friend, and when Charlie had left with his dad only the day before, that really was all Joe had been to her, albeit an old friend she was developing a major crush on. But since her son had been away, things had changed dramatically but it was so new, she didn't know what was going to happen with it herself, and she certainly wasn't ready to discuss it with her ex.

"Don't worry," said Nick, sensing her discomfort. "I know we're divorced now, and this isn't really anything to do with me. I'm not going to quiz you, though it's pretty clear he makes you happy, which I'm glad about. You deserve to be happy."

"Thanks," said Kate, gratefully.

"I have to check though: you will be careful about Charlie's feelings won't you?"

"Of course!" Kate replied, affronted. "How could you even ask me that?"

"Sorry. It's just Charlie seems to really like Joe. I don't want to see him get hurt."

"Neither do I, Nick. You know I always put Charlie first."

"Yes, I know. I guess I'm just feeling a bit . . . jealous."

Seeing her shocked look, he swiftly added, "Of Charlie spending so much time with this new chap of yours, I mean, and thinking he's so great."

"I understand, but you'll always be Charlie's dad," said Kate, relieved. "Nothing will change that, regardless of what happens between me and any other men in the future."

* * *

As much as Kate wanted to call Joe and invite him back over as soon as Nick had gone, she couldn't get Nick's words out of her head, and felt deflated and unsure. She did need to be really mindful of Charlie. He was the most important person in the world to Kate, and his thoughts and feelings had to come first. She couldn't allow herself to get too carried away in a new romance which would more than likely lead nowhere. She should proceed slowly.

So, instead of sending out the "all clear", she texted Joe to say she needed to spend the evening just with Charlie. But her resolve not to see him again that day vanished when he suggested he come over after Charlie had gone to bed, "To make sure you're tucked in properly," he wrote cheekily.

Kate and Charlie went for a walk, then had tea and did some painting together until it was time for his bath and stories. They had snuggles on Charlie's bed as Kate fiddled with his soft hair, still damp from his bath, and Charlie told her everything he'd done with Nick. He was always extra especially cuddly after being away from her for the night.

She tidied herself up, and gave the kitchen a once-over to get rid of the worst of the paint stains; how did red poster paint get everywhere, no matter how much newspaper you put down? Then, when she felt she couldn't wait any longer, she messaged Joe.

He snuck in quietly so as not to disturb Charlie, and pulled Kate to him immediately. He smelt delicious, just perfect, warm, and faintly of coffee. It felt like weeks rather than mere hours since they'd been together. Kate wasn't as nervous as she'd been the previous evening and could relax into his kisses immediately.

They went upstairs to Kate's bed, neither of them willing to put off the inevitable for a moment longer.

* * *

"Would you like a drink?" Kate asked, naked and dishevelled, propping herself up on an elbow. It was almost midnight.

"A cup of tea would be brilliant," Joe replied, stretched out beside her.

"You know, you're nowhere near as glamorous and exciting as a lot of your fans imagine," Kate teased.

"You're probably right. Can I trust you to keep my little secret? I'd hate for too many illusions about me to be shattered. I'm not sure the tabloids would be terribly interested in a quiet sort of chap who likes to drink an awful lot of tea, spend time playing with his daughter, and fit in a bit of sailing when he can. That kind of thing doesn't make the front pages."

"Do you like it?"

"The attention? The journalists and the screaming groupies?"

"Yeah."

"I guess I used to. What happened to us was like a dream. We became famous overnight at seventeen! And what seventeen-year-old doesn't dream of becoming rich and famous? But six years of touring and promoting is hard."

"Was that when your band split?"

"Yeah, we began to argue and things rapidly fell apart. Then I was offered a huge record deal as a solo artist. I hadn't made as much as you'd think in the band, but I suppose you could say I'd got used to the high life. I had a big mortgage too. I didn't know what I'd do if I didn't accept to be honest — and Genevieve pushed me into it."

"But you enjoy what you do?"

"Well, I love writing songs, that's what my real passion is. The rest of it I could happily leave behind now. I probably would have done a while ago if it hadn't been for Genevieve."

"She pushed you to continue?"

"Yeah. She's very driven. She saw us as a sort of 'power couple' — me not really wanting that didn't suit her plans. I tried to make her happy, to give her what she needed . . . but I think what it came down to is that we weren't a very good fit."

"Well," she said cautiously, "that doesn't sound like a very healthy relationship."

He nodded. "It wasn't, but us breaking up has still completely thrown me. I never imagined my marriage would end up like this. But I can't blame Genevieve; I knew what I was getting into."

"It does get easier. When my marriage collapsed two years ago, it was horrible, but once everything got sorted out with Charlie and the business, it was actually kind of a relief," Kate said.

"Did your husband want custody of Charlie?"

"I think he thought moving Charlie from his home would make the whole situation even worse. He also works away a lot, so it's more practical for Charlie to live with me, though we have shared custody. There was a small part of me that was a bit worried he'd push for Charlie to live with him, but Nick's a good guy, he wouldn't do anything to intentionally hurt Charlie or me."

"Genevieve and I haven't talked about anything like that yet. To be honest, we haven't properly talked about anything. She announced the end of our marriage rather unexpectedly."

"*She* announced it?"

"She'd been filming in France for a week or so when I had a call from my agent to tell me Genevieve had issued a statement from the both of us saying we were filing for divorce."

"She didn't discuss it with you first?"

"No, not really. The truth is I've known we wouldn't last for a long time. We both knew the other was unhappy. I think we each figured the marriage would have to end at some point, but I sort of had it in my head that we'd wait until Issy was older. Genevieve had other ideas though. For her, I suppose it was the right time for us to break up."

"That must have hurt," Kate said, though she regretted saying it at once. She didn't want to hear how heartbroken Joe was about his impending divorce, how much he missed his wife, or that she, Kate, was a rebound fling while he sorted himself out, perhaps even worked out some way to salvage his relationship.

"It did hurt," Joe admitted, "Not because of my feelings for Genevieve. I haven't loved her for a long time, but because I believed she cared about Issy, and how our separating would impact on her. I thought it was something we'd work out together to make it as non-traumatic as possible."

"I think a marriage breaking up is always going to be traumatic."

"And there's so much to sort out. I've had my stuff moved from our house; most of it's in storage in America now until I decide what to do with it. How did you sort out your business when you and Nick broke up? Especially when it's so tied up with your home. Makes it rather complicated I imagine."

"I'm buying him out. He's been very good about it really. But it's certainly not easy, is it? Breaking up a whole life you've forged with another person and starting all over again."

"Nope."

"Any idea how you and Genevieve will divide things?"

"We haven't got much together. She's worth a lot more than me so she wanted a pre-nup. It's Issy we need to sort out."

Steeling herself, Kate asked, "Well it's still early days . . . do you think you two will try to patch things up?" She felt like kicking herself as soon as she'd said it. After the amazing time they'd spent together, was she really ready to hear the answer?

He looked at her. "There's no chance of that, and I never would have started something with you if I'd thought there was the remotest chance I wasn't over Genevieve. I wouldn't do that to you, Kate. Genevieve and I had actually been basically living apart for almost a year, working on different things. The only reason Genevieve's going public now is she's in the middle of filming some blockbuster and isn't getting the publicity she hoped."

"Wow! But I'm sure I've seen photos of you two . . ."

"We were more playing the part of a happy couple for the public and Issy than actually spending time together. Genevieve did the stage managing and I turned up at a couple of events for her; we let ourselves be papped with Issy a few times for appearances."

"How come Genevieve got to call the shots?"

"You wouldn't be asking that if you'd met her," Joe laughed. "Genevieve's career means everything to her. When she and her publicist decided she needed to appeal more to the 'family' demographic . . . that's where Issy and I came into things. She soon didn't want me anymore, but threatened she'd push for full custody of Issy if I leaked we'd separated."

"That's awful!"

He shrugged sadly. "It's how it is. I shouldn't have let myself get into the situation in the first place, but I can't regret it because of Issy."

"And Issy's still staying with Genevieve?"

"Yes, they're in France: Genevieve's filming there for the next few months. To be honest, I'm not quite sure what she's up to with Issy, but I'm trusting she'll get bored of playing at being 'perfect mummy' pretty soon. I know it sounds harsh, but she doesn't like Issy cramping her style. A child doesn't really fit in with her life." He sighed, "I don't think she realised quite how much work goes into being a parent."

"Well, it's not like she had a very normal upbringing from what I've read."

"No, that's true. I suspect that's part of what drew me to her. I guess I wanted to rescue her."

She smiled. "Very noble."

"Very stupid more like." He went quiet. "Let's change the subject, this is getting depressing."

"No problem."

He cleared his throat. "Can I stay the night? If I promise to be out of the way before Charlie gets up?"

"There's nothing I'd like better," replied Kate, switching off the light by the side of the bed and tucking herself in next to him.

* * *

It took only a few moments for Joe to fall fast asleep, but Kate was kept awake by her thoughts and confused feelings about the circumstances she had unexpectantly found herself in.

For the past two years, Charlie had been enough. Kate had felt as broken as her marriage; she needed time to heal and to come to terms with her new life. She'd focused on being the best mother she could be to Charlie and making her business a success. It had taken her until now to feel like herself again, but she realised she finally did. The divorce being final had a lot to do with that, but she had to admit Joe had helped as well. Just being wanted by a man again had made her feel whole, had reawakened a part of her that had been asleep for a long time — such a long time, she'd forgotten how crucial it was to her wellbeing.

From a rather practical point of view, one day in the future, and Kate suspected that day would seem to come around far too quickly, Charlie would be grown up and she'd be left on her own. She didn't want to be. She knew it was too soon to claim Joe was the man she'd spend the rest of her life with, but it felt good to be desired.

Though desperate not to get carried away with their fledgling romance, and all too aware of what a cliché she sounded, she really had never felt this way about someone before. She'd loved Nick, of course she had, she wouldn't have married him otherwise, but her feelings for him had taken a long time to develop. What she felt for Joe was much more a bolt out of the blue, which she was still coming to terms with.

But, then again, she reminded herself, it wasn't like she and Joe were total strangers when he'd turned up on her doorstep asking to stay. The seeds of their relationship had been sown many years before. She was very unlikely to ever have that again. What if he was "the one" for her . . . if this was her chance for happiness? Surely in life you should grab opportunities with both hands?

She knew it wouldn't be plain sailing though; it wasn't like Joe didn't come with an awful lot of baggage. There was his daughter for a start. From everything Joe had said, it sounded like Issy was a lovely little girl, but who knew whether she and Charlie would get on? Or maybe Issy would hate her and resent another woman taking up her father's time. And Genevieve was quite something to live up to.

Aside from those problems, the fact would remain that the life Joe led wasn't one Kate had ever wanted. Living in the limelight and losing her freedom and privacy didn't appeal to her in the slightest, and she knew she'd struggle with it. Would she be willing to do it, if that's what it took to be with Joe? Would she be happy for Charlie to live that life too?

There were so many variables to take into account. Even just trying to list them all was making her head swim. She was usually an organised person, and liked to work things out and plan, but this was impossible. She'd just have to be brave, Kate guessed. She didn't want to give up Joe, not yet anyway, so there didn't seem any other way to go about things. She couldn't change who he was, what he did, or his ex-wife. She may as well enjoy herself and see what happens.

CHAPTER SEVEN

The next week only served to show Kate just how good she and Joe were together as they slipped further into their happy bubble of domesticity. Having Joe in her life just seemed so . . . right. So natural. Their days formed a regular routine, effortless and without drama. Joe made her feel complete and content. She was managing to hold her worries about their future at bay for the time being at least, though she did still occasionally wonder what it would be like for them when Joe's little sabbatical was over, and he was back in the "real world".

* * *

Kate was staring out of her kitchen window when Joe came up behind and put his arms around her, planting a kiss on the back of her neck.

"What are you thinking about?" he asked.

"I was looking at the garden and thinking I really need to sort out getting that leylandii in the corner cut down."

"That doesn't sound too difficult: there's plenty of room for it to fall, and the trunk doesn't look too thick," Joe said thoughtfully.

"It's not just that, the whole thing's a bit of a mess. There are a few changes I've been meaning to make for ages."

"Yeah, I remember you said something about chickens?"

"Well, perhaps that's not what I should start with . . . I need to clear some space for a veg patch if I'm going to plant anything this year, and I'd love to put in some fruit trees. And fix that rotten bit of fencing at the back. There's such a lot to do; it's hard to get motivated. And *you*," she turned to face him, "are a tiny bit of a distraction."

"Don't blame me!" Joe laughed. "Why don't I just arrange for someone to come and do it? My treat. You must know a local gardening firm you could call."

"No!" said Kate immediately, "You're not paying for my gardening to be done!"

"It could be a 'thank you' for letting me stay?"

"I'm already charging you for that!"

"See it as an extra thank you then."

"Thanks, but no. I can manage," said Kate firmly, before changing the subject. "Anyway, don't you have some songs you're supposed to be writing?"

"Are you trying to get rid of me?"

"Never," laughed Kate, "Though I need to go out soon: I'm going shopping for the day with Mum, remember?"

"Of course. I'm sure I can think of something to keep me occupied."

"I'll see you when you get back. Don't get up to any mischief while I'm gone."

"Me? Never."

* * *

Kate returned home with Charlie and her shopping at four. They carried the bags into the kitchen and were greeted, not by the usual silence of an empty house, but by Joe's frantic calls for help from upstairs. Rushing up to the landing, she found him, wet and mud-covered, firmly wedged in the tiny opening at the top of the small bathroom sash window she habitually left a little down.

"Do you know where your stopcock is?" he said, breathlessly.

"Of course I do, but what on earth are you doing?" Kate replied, trying to wiggle the jammed sash down. "Don't move!"

"I'm okay; it's a bit looser now! Go and turn the stopcock off! Quickly!"

Kate ran off downstairs and into the kitchen. Pulling a small mountain of dusters and bottles of cleaning fluid out from the cupboard under her sink, she found the stopcock and turned it clockwise. When she emerged, she heard Joe shout out, "That's done it!"

Grabbing her tool bag from the utility room, she raced back up the stairs, followed of course by Charlie, determined not to miss out on a second of the excitement.

Joe had managed to free himself, at least onto the outside windowsill. It took her a matter of moments to work the old sash low enough for him could climb through, and he finally stopped prevaricating and properly answered her increasingly irate questions: "Look, its better if I show you," he said sheepishly, "Come and see the garden."

Kate followed Joe outside, where she discovered her wild, but beautiful country garden had been transformed into something resembling the Somme. The tree she had wanted cut down was indeed down: it was on — or should that be "through", she thought — what remained of her shed and glass house. The lawn was now nothing but a muddy bog, and the fence along one side seemed to have collapsed in on itself. Inexplicably, random holes dotted the waterlogged expanse.

"What did you do?" gasped Kate, taking in the full extent of the wreckage.

"You said you didn't want me paying anyone to do the garden, but I knew how much you needed the work done, so I thought I could do it for you . . . but it turns out landscape gardening isn't really my forte . . ." Joe explained, trailing off.

Charlie had found a huge mound of, well, mud for want of a better word, and was having a lovely time jumping in it.

"This is brilliant!" he cried happily.

"Oh Charlie, you're covered in dirt!" exclaimed Kate, turning her attention to her son. "Your school uniform!"

"Sorry Mum," Charlie said, looking as shamefaced as Joe.

Sensing Kate's focus was returning to him, and he was about to hear in full her thoughts on the "job" he'd done, Joe quickly interjected, "I tried to take the tree down for you, but it fell the wrong way and landed . . . well, you can see where it landed . . . and when the shed collapsed, the tap by it must have been damaged. Water just started gushing out everywhere! I googled what to do, but I didn't have a key to the house to get to the stopcock. I thought there might be another on/off valve on the pipe somewhere, you know — where it went into the house? But I couldn't find where it went in." He pointed towards one of the holes. "I tried following the pipe back from the shed . . . but it's buried pretty deep: digging a trench was taking me forever, so I thought I'd jump along it, picking out its path with my holes . . . but I kept losing it."

His voice momentarily petered off under Kate's accusatory glare, before continuing, "Then I saw the bathroom window was open a bit. There's that soil pipe coming down the wall under it and it's right next to that big shrub-thing, so I tried to climb in . . . I got up there ok," he added defensively, "But I couldn't get the window open very wide and . . . well, I got stuck. And that's when you came home. Look, don't worry about any of it. I'm really, really sorry. I'll make it right. I'll fix it."

"I think that would be a good idea."

"But it might be sensible for me to call in some professionals to help, don't you think?"

"Yes, I do," replied Kate, stonily.

"Why don't you go back inside and have a nice cup of tea, there's bound to be some water left in the kettle?" suggested Joe. "Charlie might as well stay out here and play. It's not like he can get much muddier."

"Fine," Kate said, eyeing her filthy son with exasperation before walking back to the house. "But don't let him go anywhere near that broken glass!"

"And maybe close the kitchen blinds?" Joe called after her.

* * *

It was only thirty minutes later that Kate heard two vans from "R. Williams, Building and Gardening Services" pull into her driveway. The occupants were swiftly ushered through the gate at the side of the house.

Charlie came in soon after with the news that she could turn the water back on, and Kate began cooking a shepherd's pie, making a conscious effort not to peek through the blinds at what was going on in her garden. She even turned the radio on loud to drown out chainsaw whirring and various bangs from outside.

It was sweet of Joe to try to help; it really was, but he'd made such a mess! What had he been thinking? Her garden was destroyed!

Darkness had fallen by the time Kate heard the vans drive away, and another quarter of an hour passed before a very sorry looking Joe knocked at her front door.

"It'll all be put right by tomorrow evening," he said, exhaustedly.

"Good." She sighed. Then, "Are you sure they didn't recognise you though?" said Kate; she'd been so cross, she hadn't thought about the problem of Joe meeting with the workmen.

"Don't worry," he said, sitting down at the table, "They've signed non-disclosure forms."

"When, just now?"

"No, they did some work at my mate's house a while ago, the one I took you to. I was there at the time," Joe looked uncomfortable, but continued, "They'll be back again first thing in the morning. I thought maybe we could drop Charlie

73

at school and then go sailing together until they've finished . . ." he petered off, seeing the steely glint in Kate's eyes.

"Oh no!" she said firmly, "You're not going anywhere! I think it's a much better idea for you to keep an eye on the work and labour for them so they're done faster."

Joe knew he was beaten. "I really am sorry you know."

"I know, but I'll be more able to accept your apology when my garden doesn't look like a quagmire." Softening a little, Kate added, "I saved you some food, let me heat it up."

* * *

Kate heard the men start work at eight the next morning. She avoided looking out of the kitchen window until just before she left with Charlie and saw Joe was indeed with them, pushing a wheelbarrow around forlornly. She couldn't help but feel a little guilty at what he'd been reduced to since coming to stay with her.

She thought she could take the opportunity to give his barn a good clean when she got back. It seemed awkward to do it when he was around, but he was technically a paying guest, and, as housekeeping was included in what he was paying, she felt she should do it.

"Joe!" she called out, tapping on the window to get his attention. "Is it okay for me to pop into the barn in a bit?"

"Sure!" he shouted back.

* * *

It didn't take Kate long to whizz around the place with her duster and hoover. Joe was naturally tidy. She was used to cleaning around her guests, but it did feel different doing so with Joe's things about, and she was very conscious not to sneak a look at any of the papers on the coffee table.

She restocked the kitchen with a few essentials, though he was eating so much with her and Charlie, he didn't really need much.

Kate moved on to the barn's little garden and patio area and gave that a sweep and a tidy, weeding the pots and borders before heading back to her own house for lunch.

She was getting stuff out of the fridge when Joe popped his head around the door. "We're really getting there!" he announced, "Come and see."

Following him outside, she thought the garden did look better. At least four men were busily working. The tree was cut up ready to be taken away, and the fence fixed. The remains of the shed and glass house had been completely removed.

"The chaps are going to finish clearing the tree this afternoon and replacements are arriving for everything I broke."

"That sounds great, Joe, thanks."

"You've got to promise not to come out here again until they're done and close the kitchen blind. I've got a bit of a surprise coming for Charlie."

"That's sweet of you." Kate smiled. "I won't look, I promise."

One of the burly gardeners called, "We can do without Joe now if that's alright with you."

"Are you asking my permission for him to stop work?"

"He said you're in charge!" said the man laughing.

"Yes, he can stop now," Kate agreed magnanimously.

She failed to hide her grin at how relieved both Joe and the gardeners looked at this news. She guessed he'd been rather more of a hindrance than a help.

"Treat yourselves to a pub lunch guys," said Joe, handing them some money.

"Thanks! Come on lads. We'll be back in a while then," the foreman said, going to their vans.

Kate and Joe walked back to the house.

"Would you like something to eat?" she said.

"That would be great. Is it alright if I pop upstairs and hop in the shower first?" asked Joe, gesturing to his covering of grime.

"Please do! There's a pair of your trousers and a t-shirt by the side of my bed," said Kate laughing.

Kate was still smiling as she watched Joe disappear up the stairs. She turned the radio on and began making some sandwiches for lunch. The front door had been left unlocked, and the music meant she didn't hear it open again.

She jumped at the sound of her best friend Becca's voice calling out, "Hey there stranger!" as she walked into the kitchen.

"Hi!" Kate squeaked back.

"Are you alright?"

"Yes! Of course! Just surprised, I just wasn't expecting to see you."

"I had some time before I needed to pick the boys up from school, so thought I'd drop by and see if you fancied a coffee. It's been ages since we've had a catch-up! I texted to let you know I was on my way."

"Sorry, I haven't checked my phone, I was outside," explained Kate.

"So, are you free to pop into town for a coffee and a cake? My treat."

"I can't come right now, but I could meet you in about an hour?" suggested Kate. An hour would give her a chance to eat and explain things to Joe before going — which was infinitely preferable to chatting to Becca with Joe naked upstairs.

"Great. I need to pop to the post office anyway. Meet you at Carlo's?"

"Sounds good."

Becca was just turning to leave when Joe appeared in the kitchen doorway, wearing nothing but a rather small towel around his waist.

"I was hoping you'd join me in there," he said smiling, before noticing Becca. "Oh, um, hi," he said, blushing slightly and checking his towel was secure.

"Hi," Becca replied, a mischievous grin on her face.

"Becca, this is Joe. Joe, Becca," said Kate, inwardly cringing. "Joe's, um . . . still staying in one of the barns."

"It really is a very full service Kate offers here isn't it?" said Becca, mock-seriously.

"I'll just go and get dressed . . ." said Joe.

"Oh, please don't bother on my account; I was just on my way out. You two enjoy your . . . sandwiches," she added, spotting the plate on the side.

Kate and Joe looked at one another as Becca departed. "Hey, at least she didn't recognise you!" Kate said a little desperately. "I'm surprised to be honest; Becca loves all that Hollywood stuff. She was thrilled when I mentioned I knew you once."

"I bet you used to tell everyone you were friends with me, didn't you?" joked Joe, looking relieved.

"No. Only the very, very few people I thought might be vaguely interested when I got really, really desperate for something to talk about. Anyway, let's eat so I can get going and receive my ribbing."

Kate's mobile beeped with a message from Becca: "And of course I knew it was Joseph Wild in your kitchen. I was playing it cool."

Kate laughed and was showing Joe the message when another came through: "Okay, am done being cool! OMG!!! Hurry up so you can fill me in on EVERYTHING!"

"Can she be trusted?" asked Joe warily.

"I'd trust her with my life," Kate replied emphatically. "If I ask Becca not to tell anyone about you, she won't."

"I wish I had friends as loyal as yours."

"You do, you've got me," said Kate, reaching over and taking his hand in hers.

"How could I forget?" said Joe, leaning across the table and kissing her.

They ate, then Kate ran a brush through her hair and grabbed her handbag.

"I'll be back at about quarter to four, after I've picked up Charlie."

"Alright, I'm going to have another go at a song, I think I might actually have the beginnings of an idea."

"That's great!" said Kate, kissing Joe goodbye. "I'll see you later."

* * *

Kate was actually a couple of minutes early at the coffee shop, but Becca was already there, seated at their favourite corner table, practically beside herself with anticipation.

"Hiya," Kate said, resigning herself to Becca's inquisition. "Have you ordered coffee?"

"Nope! My treat though, and cake, in exchange for you spilling your gossip."

"I'll have a latte and a blueberry muffin then," she said, deflecting for as long as possible.

"Be right back!" Becca replied, hurrying off.

She soon returned and sat down determinedly. "Right, I want to know everything. Starting with why you didn't tell me, your closest friend, that you're sleeping with a world-famous rock star! And don't deny it!" she added quickly.

Kate looked around to check there was no one in earshot before answering quietly, "I'm not going to deny it, but you can't tell anyone, and in my defence, the sleeping together aspect of the arrangement is very new."

"How new?"

"A week and a half . . ."

"Okay, that's pretty new."

"I didn't tell you because Joe asked me not to say anything to anyone about him staying with me. He turned up out of the blue just over a fortnight ago. He needed somewhere to stay while everything calmed down with all the media craziness about him and Genevieve splitting," Kate explained.

"So he was just outside your door one day?"

"Yep. He's renting the smaller barn. Then we spent the day together sailing when Charlie was with Nick, and one thing kind of led to another . . ."

"I can't say I blame you, he's gorgeous."

"Yes, he is."

"So what's the plan for you two? Are you a couple?"

"I don't know. It's all so new, and he's only just officially separated."

"It is very soon . . ."

"Joe and Genevieve have actually been apart for a lot longer than people realise, but yeah, it is soon."

"As long as you're happy."

"I am." She paused, looking out unfocusedly over the room, weighing up her thoughts. She took the plunge, "But he was with Genevieve Moore for goodness' sake! How can I possibly hope to compare?"

"But he and Genevieve didn't work out, did they? She's obviously not the right woman for him. Maybe you are," said Becca supportively.

"I don't know what to think!" Kate burst out. "We're great together! Everything is so easy, so natural. I can't imagine him not being there, being in my life. But I'm 'me' and he's . . . well, he's a superstar!" She paused helplessly again and ran her hands through her hair.

"Is there any chance he and Genevieve will get back together?"

"He says no, but she is the mother of his child, and what if his career suffers because of their break-up? Them reuniting would certainly get plenty of publicity."

"True. But do you really think he'd get back together with her just for publicity?"

"I don't think so. I trust him. He's not . . . like you'd expect a rock star to be."

"Still, even if it doesn't last, you'll always be able to tell the grandkids you had a thing with Joseph Wild!"

"That's a fair point," said Kate laughing, though the laughter was stilted. She knew she had to be realistic about things with Joe, but she couldn't control how she felt about him, and she wasn't sure she wanted to.

* * *

Kate was glad she'd taken the time to catch up with Becca: it was good to be able to talk to her about Joe; it felt like she'd been keeping him a secret for much longer than she actually had. She wasn't a secretive person, especially when it came to her best mate.

The friends drove in their separate cars to pick up their boys from school, and said goodbye. When Kate and Charlie arrived home, the gardeners were back at work.

"Mum, why are those men still digging up our garden? I want to play football," asked Charlie, peering around the side of the kitchen blinds.

"No peeping, sweetheart," Kate reminded him, guiding him away from the window, "The men are here because Joe made a bit of a mess and it needed tidying up."

"If Joe made the mess, he should tidy it up," said the little boy seriously.

"Well, you know how sometimes your bedroom's in such a state that you need me to give you a bit of a hand with it?"

"Yep."

"It's sort of like that."

"But where is Joe? I want to show him the picture I drew at school today."

"I'm not sure. Probably in the barn."

"Can I go and see him?"

"Let's leave him for a bit. I'm sure he'll be over soon, but he was going to work this afternoon so we don't want to disturb him."

"Okay," said Charlie with a sigh.

"Pop your picture on the table and then you'll remember to show him when he comes around later."

An hour later, the workmen had left and a diffident but excited Joe came to get them both and unveil the grand works. Kate was amazed: the garden looked lovely, well beyond what she'd envisaged. There were six gorgeous new fruit trees in the corner where the leylandii had been, Charlie would love being able to pick apples and pears from them in the autumn. A beautiful oak shed, more a summer house — contemporary-looking, all thick, expertly jointed beams and clean lines — and a large, elegant glasshouse had replaced her old, decidedly ramshackle ones. The brambles and overgrowth had all been cleared and several rows of raised beds had been built, all ready for her vegetables. The concrete path had been paved with flagstones and the whole muddy shambles of a lawn had been re-turfed, all trace of holes and giant, man-made mole hills erased. Charlie came up behind her and squeaked with excitement, pointing up at the new treehouse complete with watchtower which had appeared in a low-hanging tree.

"Mum, this is amazing!" he finally managed to say once he'd climbed up the little wooden staircase to his treehouse and waved at her through its window.

"It certainly is!" Kate called back. Joe had gone above and beyond to make her garden wonderful. He must have spent a lot of money, but much more than that, it was the thought behind it all that touched her. He'd created something personal for her and Charlie, he'd understood what she'd wanted and built upon it. This wasn't just rectifying a mistake; it was a heartfelt and genuine gesture of apology.

She turned, and kissed Joe on the cheek. "Thank you" she said simply. He smiled and began to reply, "I . . ." but whatever he'd intended to say was lost as an over-exuberant Charlie came tearing into them.

* * *

Darkness fell and Kate finished preparing supper and was ready to serve up, but Joe was conspicuous by his absence. They'd parted in the garden for him to return to his composing: he was almost as overexcited about his newfound inspiration as Charlie was about the tree house. She couldn't hear the music anymore now she was inside, and thought she'd look a bit weird going out listening to check if he was still working. Kate wasn't sure what to do. She'd assumed he'd be coming over to eat, but had he actually said he was?

She wondered whether she ought to either walk to the barn to see if he was coming or just call him to find out. But would that seem too needy . . . She was fairly sure it wasn't the sort of thing Genevieve Moore would do. But then, she couldn't imagine Genevieve Moore making pie and mash either.

"Is tea nearly ready Mum?" asked Charlie, coming into the room. "I'm starving."

"Yes, sweetie. Go and wash your hands, and we'll eat in two minutes."

"But Joe's not here yet!"

"I think Joe must be busy working still. We'll just have to eat without him."

"But he'll be hungry!"

"He'll be alright love; Joe can make his own tea if he gets peckish." Kate was just placing two full plates on the table when there was a knock at the door.

"I'll get it!" shouted Charlie eagerly, throwing himself from his chair and racing to the hallway before Kate had a chance to call him back.

She wiped her hands on a tea towel and followed. The joyful cry of "Joe! My treehouse is so great!" reached her ears before she saw the man himself.

"Hey!" she said, raising her hand in greeting as Joe lifted Charlie up for a hug.

"Are you going to have tea with us, Joe? Mum's made chicken pie!" asked the little boy.

"That would be great, if I'm not too late?"

"You're just in time," said Kate.

"Thank goodness for that, I'm starving. Race you to the table, Charlie!" Joe said, putting Charlie down.

Kate followed the crazy pair back into the kitchen, wondering at how silly she'd been. Why hadn't she just called to let him know food was ready? She was so concerned with not seeming needy and not being as perfect as Genevieve, she was behaving weirdly.

Charlie chatted away nineteen to the dozen while they ate, telling them everything that had happened at school, and making plans to watch *Star Wars* with Joe at the weekend.

Yet Kate was still a little preoccupied with her own behaviour. She was usually easy-going and straightforward. Was dating a rock star going to turn her into one of those crazy women who spend their lives trying to work out what their boyfriends were thinking, worrying about every tiny thing in their relationship, and playing bizarre mind games in an effort to keep a man who really wasn't that interested in them anymore?

Joe said good night to Charlie, explaining he still had a few things he needed to finish so he had to get back to the barn. He promised Charlie extra stories the following evening and whispered to Kate that he'd return later if she wanted. She grinned at him in reply, wishing she could kiss him, but not ready to do that in front of her little boy just yet.

Charlie had an especially long bath time, involving plenty of bubbles and toys, before books and bed. Once he was settled, Kate ran a fresh bath for herself and luxuriated in the hot water and drank a glass of red wine, unwinding after the rather eventful day.

She tidied up downstairs and texted Joe to let him know to let himself in with the key left under one of the flowerpots by the front door. She'd be waiting for him in bed when he was done. She smiled at the reply that pinged through only about thirty seconds later, "I'm coming!"

Kate barely had time to give Charlie a final check to confirm he was fast asleep in his room, put on her sexiest black, lacy underwear, and light some candles, before she heard Joe turning the key in the front door.

* * *

Joe reluctantly left early again the next morning before Charlie was up. The warmth and comfort of bed was hard to abandon, but he knew Kate would rather wait a bit longer before her son learnt he was staying over.

"Sorry if I pulled you away from your work last night before you were finished," Kate said, kissing him goodbye.

"It was my pleasure to be pulled away by you."

"So, you've started writing songs again?"

"Yep! It seems I've broken through my writer's block."

"The gardening inspired you, eh?"

"You inspired me," Joe replied simply.

Kate blushed. She was speechless for a second before deciding to shrug it off. Joe had probably just been around the luvvies in Hollywood for far too long, and was used to complimenting everyone and exaggerating terribly. It was fantastic he was writing songs again, but she really doubted it had anything to do with her. It was more likely he'd just begun to relax after a stressful period of his life and that's what had kick started the creative processes again.

Sensing her disbelief, Joe came back to the rumpled bed. He sat down and leaned over, taking her gently in his arms and kissing her. Kate immediately felt self-conscious and struggled to meet his gaze.

"I'm serious," he said.

Before she could respond, they heard Charlie moving about in the next room.

"You'd better go," said Kate automatically. "Also, erm . . . there's a key for you on the kitchen table. If you'd like it."

"Wow! You're giving me a key to your house?" Joe said, beaming.

"Well, you never know when you'll need to get at my stopcock again."

He grinned. "You're amazing. Thank you. I'll see you later this evening." Chuckling, he gave her one last quick kiss.

During the day, Kate strained to hear the faint snatches of music drifting through the air randomly as she went about her tasks. She was impatient to see Joe again, her mind wandering to the previous night at any opportunity. She knew she was really falling for him, and, deep down, still wasn't sure how much of a good idea that was. But what could she do to stop herself? She hadn't planned for it to happen and had no control over her increasing affection for him. She had to be careful for Charlie's sake too, and, of course she would be. He was already so attached to Joe though, it was hard.

Joe wouldn't hurt them on purpose she was sure but . . . he had the potential to break her heart.

CHAPTER EIGHT

The following day, Joe again slipped out of Kate's bed early and returned to his barn, but he was back in the house, sat at her kitchen table, when she returned from taking Charlie to school. He was looking up charts on her laptop, searching for places they could take Charlie sailing. Kate had just gone to look for an Ordnance Survey map of the coast when she thought she heard voices.

Heading back the kitchen, keen to spend as much of the morning as she could with her man, Kate stopped dead in her tracks as she reached the doorway: sat at the table chatting to Joe was Nick.

They both turned on hearing her approach.

"Hey," Kate said awkwardly. "What are you doing here, Nick?"

"Charlie left his raincoat at my house the other day. I thought he might need it. Joseph here was just making me a cup of coffee."

Nick emphasised "Joseph", making it clear he knew precisely who Kate's "Joe" was.

Joe picked up on the atmosphere. Handing Nick a steaming mug, he said, "If you'll excuse me, I've got some stuff I need to do back at my barn."

Kate suspected Joe was bringing up the fact he was staying in the barn rather than her house for Nick's benefit, which she thought was rather sweet.

There was silence in the kitchen until Nick heard the sound of the front door closing and said, "So, Joseph Wild . . ."

"You mustn't tell anyone," said Kate quickly.

"Don't you think it would have been nice to tell me?" asked Nick grumpily.

"I promised Joe I wouldn't let anyone know he was staying here."

"I have a right to know who's living with my son."

"He's not living with us, you know that," Kate replied, becoming impatient. "He's an old friend I'm helping out. He's paying to stay in one of the barns."

"He's spending a lot of time here."

"Yes, because he's become my boyfriend. And to be honest, Nick, this is my home. I can let whoever I like visit it."

Nick knew he was beaten, but didn't look at all happy about it.

"He's a good guy," said Kate.

"I'm not saying he's not," Nick replied. "I guess it's not easy being replaced by an actual superstar who's probably worth millions."

Kate softened, understanding where her ex-husband's insecurity stemmed from. "He's not replacing you, I've told you that."

"Charlie seems to think he's pretty great."

"Charlie adores *you*. No man could ever be as important to him. Come here, silly." Kate pulled Nick to his feet and hugged him.

"His hair's a bit pretentious, isn't it?" he said quietly.

"Yes," admitted Kate with a smile. "Just a bit."

* * *

"I have a proposition for you," said Joe, when he came back round later.

"Oh yes?" she enquired, returning the kiss he gave her.

"There's a film premiere in London on Saturday, I've been offered a couple of tickets. I thought you might like to come with me." When he saw Kate's doubtful expression he added, "It's called *Just You* and it's got that Michael Gitting bloke you like in it."

"Aren't you supposed to be in hiding?"

"Yes, but I figure I can make a brief public appearance. No one will know I'm staying here. My cover won't be blown. If we take your car, we'll be completely inconspicuous."

Seeing that Kate still looked unsure, he cajoled, "Come on, you know you'll enjoy it."

"I'll enjoy the film, but I'm not sure I'm really much of a red-carpet kind of girl."

"Oh, I think you're definitely a red-carpet kind of girl. I for one won't be able to take my eyes off you."

"I'll trip over and fall flat on my face," said Kate, struggling to remain serious.

"No you won't. I'll be with you the whole time."

"I just don't think it'll be my kind of thing . . ."

"You won't know until you've tried it."

"Couldn't you go without me?"

"I could, but the entire point is to take you. And think about it this way, if I did feel forced to go by myself, I'll be surrounded by all sorts of beautiful women, who'll think I'm single. I'll be so busy fighting them off, I won't get to see any of the movie."

"My goodness you think a lot of yourself," Kate teased.

"Maybe, but are you sure it's a risk you're willing to take?" Joe pulled Kate to him, brushing a strand of hair from her cheek gently, and kissed her. Feeling her continued reluctance, he suggested, "Look, what if we sneak you in after me? We'd still get a little break together and you'd still get to see the film, but you wouldn't have to do the red-carpet rubbish and no one would get any photos of you."

"That sounds better," she conceded.

"We'll even come up with a cover story for you if you want, you could be my new personal assistant?" Sensing her wavering, he added, "It would be our little secret just how *personal* your assistance is."

"Alright," Kate agreed with a snort. "As long as I don't get photographed."

"Would it really be so terrible if people knew we were together?" said Joe, sounding hurt.

"At the moment, yes. I'm not ready for my life to become public property, and Charlie certainly isn't."

"Well, dating me, it kind of comes with the territory," he apologised.

"I know. And that's something I'm trying to come to terms with." She hesitated, wanting to be honest, but also not wanting to rebuff him, "But it's still a bit soon. I've got Charlie to think about, and you and I have only just got together."

He grinned at her. "We may have only just got together, but I've been dreaming about kissing you since that first English lesson. I'm in this for the long haul."

Kate smiled back, but her mind was in turmoil: what Joe said was lovely, and she cared for him a lot, she really did, but how could she absolutely guarantee that what she felt wasn't just a crush on a very good-looking, very famous rock star? For heaven's sake: millions of women across the world fancied him! She couldn't turn her life, and more importantly, Charlie's life, upside down, for an infatuation! What sort of mother would that make her? And what would the papers say? As far as they were aware, Joe and Genevieve had only just broken up; everyone would assume she played some part in it and had stolen Joe away from his loving family!

Her head told her she needed more time to get to know Joe properly, and work out if he truly was as perfect for her as her heart said he was. She had too much to risk if she rushed things.

But she did love the idea of a mini-break with Joe, and seeing the film would be fun. And he was right: she didn't fancy the idea of him being alone at the premiere among all those gorgeous film stars. It wasn't that she didn't trust Joe

— she did — but putting your boyfriend in a building filled with some of the most beautiful women in the world, who were all under the impression he was very much available, was asking just a bit too much.

* * *

Susie readily agreed to babysit for the weekend, in no small part helped by Kate's promise that she'd finally give in and let her meet — and be allowed to gush over — her daughter's "superstar boyfriend". And she was almost beside herself with excitement at the thought of Kate mixing with celebrities, though most put out to hear Kate's face wouldn't be plastered across the tabloids the morning after the premiere. Kate explained her reasoning, but her mum only commented, "I'm sure I was never as sensible as you when I was your age."

"You make it sound like a criticism!"

"Not at all, darling! I'm very proud of you: I can't imagine many women in your situation being so cautious. You're an amazing mum, Charlie's very lucky."

"Thank you," Kate replied, self-consciously going silent for a moment, "It helps I've absolutely no desire to be famous; I can't think of anything worse than having my every move scrutinised and reported on."

"But what if that's what it'll take to be with Joe?"

Kate again fell quiet, "I'm still working on that one."

"You'll sort something out."

"I hope so Mum, I really do."

* * *

Kate drove them both to London on Friday: they left early after she'd dropped Charlie off at school. Joe had booked a room for them in the Dorchester, and they planned to drive back home late after the premiere the following day so they'd be able to relax for a few hours before spending Sunday afternoon with Charlie.

Kate had searched and searched her wardrobe the evening before they left to find something suitable to wear to a major film premiere in the heart of London's West End. Nothing she had seemed quite right, but there was no time to buy anything else, so she ended up packing a couple of options, and planned to make the final decision on the night. They'd have time on Saturday to look around the shops, she consoled herself. Maybe she'd find the perfect dress then.

She enjoyed the drive. She and Joe never seemed to run out of things to talk about, and it was quite refreshing to have a passenger who wasn't asking "Are we nearly there yet?" every few minutes and didn't require supervision in the loos at the services when they stopped.

Still, her beloved Charlie was never far from her mind and she was already planning what present she could bring him back from London before they'd even entered the city.

Joe directed Kate to the Dorchester, a hotel usually far out of her price bracket. When Joe had said he'd book a room, Kate had immediately offered to pay half, but he'd refused, "I want to treat you," he said. "The Dorchester is my favourite hotel in London by far, but it's expensive. I want you to experience it, but I'd feel bad if you paid towards it."

"I've never stayed there," admitted Kate. "But I'd love to. Thank you."

When they actually arrived at the hotel, it turned out Joe had arranged for them to have a suite complete with butler service and a view of Hyde Park. Kate began to protest, but Joe stopped her firmly, "I said I wanted to treat you," he said, kissing her.

Joe had made the booking under a false name, but she thought the staff must surely realise who he was nonetheless. However, if they did, they all remained professionally ignorant.

As they were shown to the lift by the concierge, Kate noticed they were being watched by two absolutely enormous men, standing on opposite sides of the lobby, both equally imposing and not a little bit scary. They appeared supremely out of place in the ornate, grand surroundings of a luxury hotel.

Joe spotted Kate looking at them, "They're with me," he whispered, "My bodyguards, they've been tailing us since Reading services."

"You have bodyguards?"

"Sometimes unfortunately, yes. I started off determined to do without them, but I had a couple of rather unpleasant experiences, so now, with Issy to think about as well, it seems sensible, if a little embarrassing."

"They're big guys."

He laughed. "That's the idea."

"And they'll be right outside our hotel room?"

"They're slightly more subtle than that. They're staying in a room close by. I can just give them a call if there's anything worrying us."

"Don't you find it a bit strange, having them following you all the time?"

"I try not to think about it. I guess it is strange, but if I'm in London or LA with Issy in particular, having them around is reassuring. Sadly I've learnt there are some disturbed people in the world, and I'd never forgive myself if someone hurt Issy just because of who I am," Joe explained. "They're very tactful, and they're really nice guys."

Sensing Kate still wasn't feeling exactly calmed by this, he added, "Just try not to dwell on it. You won't see them much anyway, I promise. But it's probably best we stick to our room this evening and order in some room service. The staff here are very discreet, but I'm not sure the same can be said for its patrons. I don't fancy spending dinner being gawped at. Keeping out of the spotlight for a bit has made me fully appreciate my privacy: it's going to be hard to go back."

Kate squeezed his hand reassuringly. "Room service sounds great."

The concierge showed them to their suite then opened the door and stood aside. Kate did her best to appear as if she stayed in places like the Dorchester all the time and tried to take it all in as surreptitiously as possible.

The space was massive. They were in a wood-panelled sitting room, containing sumptuous looking sofas and a dining area complete with chandelier, and there seemed to be extra rooms everywhere. Her eyes were immediately drawn to the fresh flowers beautifully displayed on a table by a huge floor to ceiling window, through which Hyde Park tempted.

"Would you like some help unpacking, sir? Madam?"

"No thank you," replied Joe, subtly handing the man a tip, "But the clothes in the suit carrier could do with pressing, and we'd love a pot of tea."

"Of course, sir."

Kate, determined to maintain the appearance of being blasé, pretended to be absorbed in her mobile while Joe finished off with the concierge. She surreptitiously took some photos and messaged them to Becca. What she desperately wanted to do was to wander around the suite, nosing in all the drawers, cupboards and wardrobes.

"Are you sure you don't mind eating in here tonight?" Joe asked once they were alone.

"Are you kidding me? Of course not! I've never been in such a gorgeous place; I want to make the most of it."

He smiled. "Great. Why don't you run yourself a bath and relax?" he suggested. "I've got a few phone calls to make about tomorrow night."

"Okay, see you in a bit," said Kate happily. The bedroom had a luxurious king-sized bed and more stunning views of the park. The enormous main bathroom was even more lavish, the grandeur of which seemed to outstrip even that of the rest of the suite. Everywhere gleamed. A huge claw-footed bath stood in the centre of the marble room. Thick, soft, white towels warmed on a rail, and a selection of bathing goodies was displayed on the units in between two large sinks. Kate smiled to herself; she could definitely get used to this!

She stripped and ran a deep, hot bath. Embracing the spirit of decadence, she added the whole of the complimentary bottle of divine smelling bubble bath. As she climbed in, she could hear Joe talking on the phone and she smiled. She liked having him close by.

* * *

Pink and glowing, Kate finally dragged herself from the tub, walked back into the bedroom, and stopped dead. Awaiting her was a Temperley gown: strapless, full length and silver, even lying on the bed it seemed to glimmer as it caught in the light. A dress worthy of any A-lister. And next to it, strappy silver high-heeled shoes with tell-tale Louboutin red soles.

Unwrapping her towel, she slid the dress over her head: it floated down around her and slid itself into place. It fitted perfectly.

Joe came in behind her. "Do you like it?" he asked quietly.

"Of course I do, it's completely gorgeous! But where did it come from? And how did you know my size?"

"Let's just say I called in a few favours and did a little investigating of the clothes you left on the floor the other night!"

"It's amazing! I feel like, well, like a celebrity I suppose!"

"Good. You look fantastic."

"Thank you." Kate couldn't help a twirl, then froze. "I'd better take it off now though before I damage it."

"That I can definitely help you with," said Joe, a mischievous grin on his face.

* * *

The next day the reality of where she was going was beginning to sink in. She'd never done anything remotely like this before. So far their trip had been completely free of media attention, but that was because they'd been confined to the hotel room. Joe had suggested she go out for a while, but she wanted to be with him, and if he went into central London, he was bound to be recognised, and then they wouldn't get any peace. A bit of investigating, and the press might even discover where he was staying.

The suite was sumptuous and spending a morning in it with Joe wasn't exactly a hardship, but it had given her an idea of what life as "Joseph Wild's girlfriend" would be like, and there were aspects of it which didn't appeal to Kate in the least. She wanted to be able to pop out to the shops whenever she needed to. She didn't want to have bodyguards following her and Charlie every time they went out in public. But would she be prepared to put up with all that if it meant being with Joe?

The man himself came into the bedroom, breaking her thoughts.

"You're beautiful," he said simply.

"It's a beautiful dress," replied Kate, blushing.

"I'm not interested in the dress," Joe said, kissing her. "Are you almost ready? The car will be here soon."

"Yep. I just want to give Charlie a quick call, to say good night."

"I'll let the guys know we'll be ready to leave soon, see you in a minute."

He kissed her again before leaving her to phone her son.

Charlie was having a wonderful time with Susie and chatting with him allayed any feelings of guilt she had for going away and leaving him behind.

There was a knock on the door of the suite soon after she'd finished her call. Kate joined Joe and they went downstairs together, flanked by the bodyguards Kate did her best not to be bothered by. Joe took her hand with a smile to help her in her heels.

"Would you rather I'd got you flats?" he asked, jokingly.

"No way. If I'm going to do this, I'm going to do it properly. This may be the only premiere I ever go to."

"Not if I've got anything to do with it," said Joe.

"Your car is ready for you, Sir," said the smiling concierge as they entered reception.

"Thank you," replied Joe, and they continued outside to where a huge, black stretch limo, a car directly out of every news report on every film premiere Kate had ever watched, was waiting with the driver standing patiently beside it to help them in. Kate resolved to make the very most of the afternoon and evening before her.

* * *

Joe squeezed Kate's leg, checking she was alright as their limo pulled up in front of the cinema. There was a large crowd gathered outside and their car joined a queue comprised almost entirely of vehicles identical to their own. As they inched slowly forwards, the sound of the crowd grew louder, and the butterflies in Kate's stomach were going crazy. She watched out of the window as each car halted, its back door was opened, and various celebrities emerged. It really was like seeing it happen on the television.

When it was their turn, the limo stopped and Joe gave her a quick kiss on the cheek. "See you inside," he said. He took a second, steeling himself, plastered a smile on his face just as the door was opened for him, and stepped out into the mayhem. Kate had a few very uncomfortable seconds of feeling like a rabbit in the headlights, with the cameras flashing and fans screaming once they realised who was now amongst them.

"You okay there, love?" asked the chauffeur.

"I think so. It's a bit crazy, isn't it?" Kate replied slowly.

"Sure is! But this is nothing; you should have seen it when the new *Star Wars* film premiered. Now that was crazy," he replied cheerfully. "You ready?"

"As I'll ever be."

Kate stepped out into the wave of light and noise, trying to make herself look as small and insignificant as possible. A group of people all talking on their phones stood to one side, next to the metal barriers, and she joined them figuring there was safety in numbers. Though she needn't have worried:

with the car's celebrity passenger already disembarked, anyone now emerging was "entourage" and was largely disregarded, the throng's attention already moving on to the next car in the queue.

A small, rather harassed looking woman looked up from her phone and came to stand next to her. "Kate?"

"Yes."

"I'm Emily, publicist. Come with me."

Kate followed Emily along the red carpet and was thankfully completely ignored by the reporters and photographers. She felt like she was in a bubble, surrounded by the shouting and cheers, but not actually part of it. They went in the front entrance, swallowed by the relative silence, and through several passages until they reached the auditorium. "Here's your seat," said Emily casually, and then left.

A few other people wandered around, some clearly cinema staff from their uniforms, others presumably hangers on, much like herself, who kept themselves amused by taking selfies. She began to wish she'd brought a book with her. She had a few glances her way, but everyone else swiftly realised she wasn't a celebrity and went back to their phones.

Eventually, more people began to troop in, including Joe, who sat down next to Kate. "Are you alright?" he whispered to her.

"Er . . . yes, I think so," she replied. "It's pretty weird, to be honest."

"Just enjoy the film," he advised. "There aren't any photographers in here, so you can relax. I'm afraid it doesn't look like Michael's coming in."

"Why not?"

"He's probably seen the film a few times, and after shooting it for months, I imagine he's sick of the thing. I saw him settling himself at the bar downstairs."

Kate did her best to follow Joe's advice, though she struggled to really concentrate on the director's introduction and the screen, especially as the lights dimmed and Joe put his arm around her. It felt lovely, but she couldn't help feeling watched, and she couldn't relax.

* * *

Kate and Joe left by the back entrance, where their car, bodyguards and driver all awaited them. It was only a short journey to Soho where everyone was meeting, in a bar so hip they had to walk down an alleyway to an unmarked, almost hidden door to find it.

They were ushered straight in by the doorman to a packed, animated throng. The lighting was dim and Francoise Hardy was just audible in the background.

"Let me introduce you to Michael," offered Joe, taking her hand and steering her through everyone towards where the actor stood, surrounded by a sea of fluttering women.

Michael spotted Joe approaching and welcomed him with a cheerful, "Hey dude, what's up?" as he wiped away some rather suspicious white powder from beneath his nose. He certainly wasn't nearly as polished looking close up as he was on screen. In fact, Kate thought he looked in need of a good scrub and a hot meal.

"Congratulations on the movie," Joe said.

"Aw, thanks, man."

"This is my friend, Kate," introduced Joe.

"What's up, babe?" Michael said to Kate, with a slight leer and unfocused eyes. She recoiled somewhat: talk about destroying a fantasy.

"I'm off to the bathroom, wanna come?" he asked Kate suggestively.

"Er, no thanks, I'm okay," she replied, feeling Joe's body stiffen beside her protectively.

"Suit yourself," replied Michael with a shrug before turning and veering off in the direction of the restroom.

"Yikes," Kate muttered under her breath.

"Um, sorry about that! Movie stars eh?" said Joe, looking embarrassed. "Shall we get a drink?"

"Yep. I think I need one."

They turned, and Kate suddenly found herself facing a tall, immaculate blonde she immediately recognised as Genevieve Moore. Stunningly dressed in a white, sequinned jumpsuit, her long, silky hair cascaded down her shoulders; the term Ice Queen came instantly to mind. Kate tried to make eye contact and smile at Genevieve but was firmly ignored.

"Presumably this is who you've been hiding out with," said Genevieve, not even bothering to hide her sneer as she looked down at Kate. Resisting her natural reaction to shrink away, Kate made herself meet the hostile glare.

"Genevieve, I wasn't expecting you to be here, I thought you were still in France," said Joe, kissing her on the cheek. "Kate's an old friend of mine. I've been renting a place from her. I told your assistant where I was. Did she forget to let you know?"

In ordinary circumstances, Kate would have moved out of earshot of what was shaping up to be a private argument, but might Joe want her support? Genevieve's disdain settled it. She stayed.

"She may have mentioned you weren't at the beach house," replied Genevieve offhandedly, continuing to shoot daggers at Kate.

"How's Issy?" Joe asked.

"Ismene is fine, if more than a little demanding. She doesn't seem to understand the importance of my work, or how much it takes out of me."

"She's five," replied Joe curtly. When Genevieve didn't respond he followed with, "Is Issy still in France?" his tone clipped.

"Oh no, she's here."

Seeing Joe look around, Genevieve added, "Not actually here, obviously. She's in London."

"Well, can I see her?"

"Call my assistant tomorrow, she'll arrange something. She knows my schedule. I'm afraid I really must go and mingle," and before Joe could comment, she turned and dis-appeared into the crowd.

Kate noticed quite a number of people had drawn in to watch the exchange. The event over, they began to drift away, muttering excitedly to one another.

"So . . ." said Joe, running his fingers through his hair, "That was Genevieve."

"She seems quite a . . . force to be reckoned with."

"That's one way of putting it."

Joe was clearly distracted as he took Kate's hand.

"Are you alright?" she asked softly.

"I just can't believe Issy's in London and Genevieve didn't tell me. Though I don't know why I'm surprised."

"Do you think you'll get to see her?"

"I'll call Genevieve's assistant tomorrow. As instructed. If I don't get anywhere with her, I'll contact my lawyer I guess and see what he suggests."

Kate squeezed his hand. "Would you like to leave?"

"No, no. I'm not going to let Genevieve spoil your evening."

"She hasn't, I promise," said Kate. "But it's getting late and we've got a long drive ahead of us. Anyway, don't you think being alone together back home sounds more fun?"

"It does indeed," said Joe smiling. He took out his phone, "I'll call for the car."

* * *

Their driver dropped them back at the Dorchester where Kate's Renault Clio was waiting, ready packed with all their stuff.

Joe went quiet after they were out of London. Kate assumed he was asleep, and was listening to the radio when he said, "Kate, be honest, was this evening really awful for you?"

"No," Kate replied carefully. "Not awful, but I think I was right when I said premieres really aren't my thing."

Joe was silent again and Kate, worried she'd offended him, added, "I so appreciate all the effort you went to though: I loved the hotel and I love spending so much time with you. And the dress and shoes you bought me are absolutely amazing."

Joe smiled sadly. "I'm really sorry about Genevieve being there tonight. I had no idea she would be. I thought she was still in France."

"Don't worry, I know you didn't plan for me to bump into her, but it was pretty awkward."

"It certainly was."

"Do you think she knows something's going on between us?"

"No, but she suspects."

"I hope it won't cause you trouble."

"I'll be fine. Genevieve's in absolutely no position to complain about me dating anyone. It's you I'm worried about."

"Don't be, I'm okay. It was just a completely bizarre situation."

"Has it put you off me?" asked Joe quietly.

"Of course not!" Kate replied quickly. "Though to be honest the last couple of days have made me more aware of what it's like to live your life, and what it would mean for me, and for Charlie, to be a part of it." She felt very self-conscious, though somehow it was easier to say these things when she couldn't look Joe in the eye but had to keep watching the road.

"There was so much I hadn't considered," she continued. "Bodyguards for goodness' sake! How do you cope with living like that? I mean you were visiting London, but you couldn't leave your hotel room most of the time!"

"You get used to it. And don't forget everything is crazier than usual at the moment. I'm sorry you didn't get to go out and explore."

"That didn't matter: I can visit London anytime. I wanted to spend the time with you, and the suite was fantastic. It was more the fact that we *couldn't* do things rather than that we didn't, if that makes sense."

"It's not normally such a problem, especially if I'm by myself and I wear sunglasses and a cap."

"I don't want to have to wear sunglasses and a cap when I leave the house, and I don't want Charlie to have to either! It's not a life I'd ever choose for us."

He didn't respond immediately. Finally, he asked, "Is this your way of telling me you want to break up with me?"

"No! It's my way of telling you I'm confused," Kate tried to explain. "A few weeks ago I didn't imagine I'd ever see you again, let alone that we'd be having this conversation."

"So what do you want to do?"

Kate hesitated. Rain began to fall and she absentmindedly turned on the wipers, the headlights of the cars in the opposite lane distorted in the streaked tracks. Honestly, what did she really want?

"For now, I just want to enjoy being with you. My mum isn't bringing Charlie back until tomorrow lunchtime. Let's make the most of it."

"That sounds good. And we'll sort this all out somehow; we're too perfect together not to."

Kate wanted more than anything at that moment to be able to agree with Joe, to see things as simply as he did, but she just couldn't. As much as she desired him, and as important and integral to her world as he was already, she found it more impossible than ever to imagine a way they could have a future together. Their lives were so far apart, could they ever meet in the middle?

CHAPTER NINE

Joe stayed over at Kate's house that night. They hadn't got back until after two and had headed straight to bed, planning a long lie-in, but it was only just gone eight thirty in the morning when the doorbell rang.

"Who on earth can that be at this time on a Sunday?" asked Joe, disorientated.

"No idea. Mum wouldn't be bringing Charlie back this early; she said she was taking him out swimming. They shouldn't be back until about three," Kate said, pulling on her dressing gown.

She hurried down the stairs. The doorbell was being rung almost constantly now. Whoever was outside wasn't feeling particularly patient it seemed.

Kate blearily answered the door and found herself facing a fresh-faced, and once again immaculate, Genevieve.

The actress had her hair pulled back in a ponytail and sunglasses resting on top of her head, despite the somewhat dreary weather. She wore skin-tight skinny jeans and a pale pink cashmere jumper. Her skin was perfect; yet she didn't look like she was wearing much make-up.

Kate pulled her tatty dressing gown closer around herself.

"Oh, it's you," Genevieve said scornfully. "I'm looking for Joseph. I've been to the address he left for me, but he's either not answering the door, or isn't in."

Joe chose that moment to appear at the top of the stairs. He'd tugged on a pair of jeans, but his top half was bare. "I thought that was your voice, Genevieve," he said wearily.

The movie star's eyebrows rose with exaggerated drama, "Ah, there you are. Been making the most of the local attractions I see."

"Daddy!" called out a little voice, and a small figure appeared from behind Genevieve. Kate recognised Joe's daughter Ismene immediately from the many newspaper and magazine photos the little girl had featured in.

Ismene ran past Kate to her father, who'd now made his way to the bottom of the stairs. Joe scooped her up easily in his arms. "Issy darling, I've missed you so much!" he said.

"I've missed you too, Daddy!"

He carried her back to the door.

"What's going on, Genevieve?" he asked his soon-to-be-ex-wife.

"You said you wanted to see your daughter."

"Of course I want to see her, but some warning would have been nice. How did you even get here at this time in the morning? You must have been up before dawn."

"You know I've always been an early riser," said Genevieve dismissively. Joe didn't look convinced. "I'm going back to France later today. Ismene says she's been missing you. I've got a lot of work to do, and frankly it would be much easier for me to do it without a child in tow. She can either stay here or come with me, it's your choice."

"Please can I stay Daddy?" asked Issy.

"I think that would be a great idea," Joe replied, smiling down at his daughter.

"Good," said Genevieve. "Her stuff's in the car. I can't hang around: some of us have a job to do and don't have the luxury of spending all day lounging around in our pyjamas." She looked at Kate pointedly.

"Would you mind watching Issy for a minute while I speak to her mother outside?" Joe asked Kate, glaring at Genevieve. Now that he wasn't completely focused on his daughter, he looked livid. Kate had never seen him like this. She may not have been close to Joe for quite some time, but Kate suspected it took a lot to push him to this point.

"Of course," she answered quickly, offering her hand to Issy, who stared at it suspiciously. "Would you like some juice?" Kate asked, hoping to win over the little girl.

"Ismene doesn't drink juice," snapped Genevieve. "It would rot her teeth."

"So sorry," muttered Kate under her breath before suggesting, "How about water then?"

Genevieve ignored her and turned back to Joe. Kate took this as the hint that she should get on with taking Ismene out of the way.

Leading Issy into the kitchen, Kate got her a glass of water. Genevieve's voice rose indistinctly in the background. Ismene sat prettily at the table, perfectly poised and expressionless, observing her hostess. She was certainly a very beautiful child; she had her mother's huge eyes and thick blonde hair, but something of Joe in the line of her jaw and the symmetry of her face.

"So . . ." began Kate, trying to think of a conversation she could start up. Small boys she knew how to talk to, but girls were another matter. Thankfully Joe came in, still looking wound up.

"Mummy's leaving now," he said to his daughter. "Let's go and say goodbye."

Not quite certain what to do with herself, Kate followed the pair back outside.

Genevieve signalled to the car in the driveway and the driver got out and opened the boot. He brought over two large suitcases and dropped them in front of Joe with as much disdain as his mistress herself would have.

"I'll be going then," announced Genevieve breezily. "Be good, darling," she said to her daughter, blowing her an air kiss. "Any problems, call my assistant."

With a final waft of perfume, she turned and was back in the car. It drove off quickly, leaving a cloud of dust behind it.

Issy didn't seem at all bothered that her mother was leaving. She cuddled into her daddy, looking exhausted.

"Shall I make us some breakfast?" Kate suggested pragmatically.

"Would you mind if I just took Issy to the barn and got her settled in?" Joe asked.

"Not a problem," said Kate. Of course she was disappointed her romantic morning was wrecked, but she more than understood. And it was lovely to see Joe reunited with his daughter again. It just made her angry to think how Genevieve had manipulated the situation.

"Ok, thanks. I'll see you later, yeah?"

"Yep. Why don't we all have dinner together tonight?"

"That would be great," said Joe, sounding relieved she wasn't cross with him. Living with Genevieve must have been a minefield of emotions, Kate thought.

She went back into the house and made herself a cup of tea and a slice of toast and honey while she decided what to do with her day until Charlie arrived home, and Joe and Issy came for dinner. It occurred to her she had no idea what she could possibly make for Issy: she'd read numerous articles over the years about Genevieve's passion for cooking, and how she insisted her daughter ate a totally macrobiotic, gluten-free, vegan diet, and had done since birth. The child had probably never even been in the same room as a packet of Haribo, let alone eaten any. Kate was pretty decent in the kitchen but she wasn't even entirely sure just what a macrobiotic meal would consist of. Thank goodness she had a few hours to find out! She could look up some recipes on the internet, but if Issy was going to be staying for a while, a proper book on what she'd be able to eat would be helpful. She wanted Joe's daughter to feel comfortable in her home, and she certainly couldn't have the poor little mite going hungry.

She quickly showered and dressed and headed into town. There was a Waterstones on the high street that must have a suitable cookbook, then she could pop to the supermarket and pick up any ingredients she didn't have in.

It didn't take long for Kate to spot the perfect book on the shelves: *Eat Well for Happiness*, written by none other than Genevieve Moore herself. Though Kate couldn't help smiling as she read the introduction where Genevieve described why she and her daughter followed the strict diet they did, and how she'd even managed to convince her husband to give up his beloved British pie and mash in favour of her food. It certainly didn't look that way from what she'd seen, thought Kate, snorting.

Flicking through the pages, she had to confess nothing looked overly appetising, but it would be what Issy would find familiar and so be most comfortable with. After some deliberation, she chose a main course, two side dishes and a pudding she thought she could cope with. Once her purchase was completed, she headed to the supermarket for the supplies. And then to the closest health food shop, another half an hour's drive away, when the supermarket didn't stock half the ingredients she needed.

Some of the recipes needed a fair amount of preparation so drawing up a mental to-do list, she allowed herself just a ten-minute break for a sandwich when she got back home before starting cooking, and texted her mum to ask her to keep Charlie for a while longer.

* * *

By the time Susie arrived with Charlie, Kate was exhausted and thoroughly fed up with cooking. Everything was so fiddly and took so long.

"My goodness, you've been busy," Susie said, following Charlie into the house. Charlie flung himself into his mother's arms and began telling her all about his many adventures since he'd last seen her.

"It certainly sounds like you've had a good time!" said Kate when he'd finally finished.

"Yep! Now I'm going to get my football and play with Joe!"

"Is Joe here?" asked Susie, checking her reflection in the side of the kettle and smoothing her hair down.

"No, I'm afraid not, he's over in the barn," said Kate, "Joe will see you a bit later, sweetheart. Would you take your bag upstairs for me please?"

"Yes, Mum!" said Charlie cheerfully and he began to lug his rucksack out of the room.

"How was London? Tell me all about it! Did you meet anyone famous?" said Susie.

"I met Genevieve."

"No! What was she doing there? I thought she was in France."

"So did Joe. Apparently she just had to pop over to the UK for that premiere!"

"What did you think of her?"

"She seemed pretty horrid!" Kate paused for a second, wondering whether she was perhaps being a little hard on the woman "In her defence, I didn't see her for very long, and for most of that time she was talking to Joe. She's certainly very beautiful, but definitely used to having her own way. I don't think she was too impressed with me."

"In what way?" asked her mother, offended.

"I don't think she was very pleased I was with Joe."

"Well that's just ridiculous; she's got her own new man now anyway according to the papers, some Russian body-builder. Pay no attention to the silly woman. Forget about her."

"That's exactly what I'd planned to do, until she turned up here this morning."

"What?!"

"She'd decided it was time Joe got to see his daughter."

"Ismene was here as well?"

"She still is, Genevieve left her with Joe."

"Things have been busy."

Kate sighed. "You could say that."

"So, why all the cooking?"

"I invited Joe and Issy for dinner, before thinking about what I would feed the child who apparently only eats seaweed and pulses."

"This does all look very healthy," said Susie, encouragingly.

"Yes . . . but will it taste any good?"

"I'm sure it will, your cooking's always lovely."

"Thanks, Mum."

Susie glanced around. "Do you need a hand?"

"I'm alright; I've done nearly all the preparation now."

"Well, if you're sure, I'll get back home and put my feet up, that little monkey of yours has tired me out."

"Oh, he wasn't naughty for you was he?"

"Not at all, he was an angel, just busy."

"That's Charlie!"

"I'll see you soon, love. Say hello to Joe for me, won't you?" added Susie.

"Of course, I will."

Charlie re-emerged to have a goodbye hug and kiss from Granny. Once the excitement of her departure was over and his attention was back on his surroundings, he examined what Kate was preparing.

"What's this?" he said, suspiciously prodding a stick of okra.

"We've got guests for tea so I'm making something special."

"Oh," was the reply. He didn't appear at all convinced by this turn of events. "Granny took me to McDonalds."

"That was nice of her."

"They had burgers. I like burgers."

"I know you do."

"You could make burgers!" he said hopefully.

"I will soon, but not tonight. Actually, our guests will be here in a minute, can you guess who they are?" Kate asked, trying to take her son's focus away from the unusual food he'd soon be facing.

"Is it Joe?"

"Yes, but there's someone else as well: Joe's little girl Issy has come to stay."

"Issy's here!" said Charlie excitedly.

"Yep, her mum's had to go and work in France again, so Issy's come to be with her dad."

"Can we go and see her now? I want to play football with her!"

"Not right now because I need to finish making dinner, but she'll be here very soon."

"I've got to get my toys ready!" said Charlie, and promptly raced back up the stairs again.

Joe and Issy arrived at six. Charlie exuberantly came down to greet them, but the sight of the legendary Ismene caused him to lose his nerve, and he ended up muttering a quick "Hi," before taking hold of his mother's hand and looking rather embarrassed.

"Hello Issy," said Kate.

Issy gave a shy smile but remained silent. Joe spoke for them both and explained how she'd slept for most of the morning and then they'd relaxed together for the remainder of the day.

"Charlie, how about you take Issy into the garden and show her your treehouse?" suggested Kate in an attempt to break the ice and help the children overcome their reserve.

"Okay," Charlie said quietly. "Come on," he called to Issy. She tentatively took his outstretched hand and allowed herself to be led outside.

"Are you sure you're alright with all this?" Joe asked anxiously, once the children were out of hearing and gesturing towards where Issy had gone.

"Of course!" replied Kate immediately. "It's great she's here. I've been dying to meet her."

"This didn't exactly fit in with our plans for today though, did it?"

"No, but that's what happens when you've got kids."

"That's true, thanks for being so welcoming to Issy. As you can see, she's pretty shy."

"So was I at that age, and I'm sure Charlie will bring her out of her shell," Kate said, giving Joe a reassuring kiss.

"Can I help with anything?" he asked, looking around and smelling the unusual aromas hanging in the air. "What's cooking?"

"Some of Genevieve's recipes actually, I wanted to make sure I made something Issy would eat so I went into town and bought Genevieve's book. I hope I've done everything as Issy likes it, it's not anything I've eaten before."

"Oh . . . I'm sure everything's delicious, though . . . er . . ." Joe began, but he was interrupted by the children coming back in, "Guess what, Mum!" Charlie said, "Issy said my tree house is the best tree house she's ever seen!"

"That's great sweetheart," Kate said. "I think it should be ready to dish up now, so why don't you both go and wash your hands? You can go and play outside again after food."

Kate brought the serving dishes to the table. She couldn't help but notice neither of the children looked very pleased, and Joe had a strange, overly-cheerful smile on his face. She was also fairly sure he was nudging Issy under the table as she kept looking down at her legs and then back up at her dad in confusion.

"Right, Issy," Kate said. "Let me see to you first . . ."

She held up a spoonful of pickled artichoke to put on the little girl's plate, Issy looked terrified.

"What's that?" she asked weakly.

"It's pickled artichoke. Doesn't it look like when your mum makes it for you?" Kate said, getting the cookbook from the countertop and flicking to the page with the recipe on. There was a large photo of the dish on the facing page; she thought it looked just like what she'd prepared.

"Your mum says it's your favourite. See, right here!" Kate said pleadingly, pointing to the relevant paragraph.

"It looks a bit weird," said Issy, clearly trying to be as polite as possible in the circumstances.

"Kate, it was so good of you to go to so much trouble, but the thing is, not everything in Genevieve's book is strictly . . . correct," explained Joe.

Kate was confused. "What?"

"Guys," said Joe, turning to the children. "Can you two go and play in the sitting room for a couple of minutes while we get the food sorted out?"

Charlie and Issy got down from the table with relief and wandered into the next room.

"What you need to understand about Genevieve is that she isn't really 'her' a lot of the time," Joe explained.

Kate look perplexed so he continued, "'Genevieve Moore' is a product. She has a whole team of people deciding how she should look, how she should act, and what she should say. She didn't really have very much to do with that book at all from what I remember — she certainly didn't actually write it."

"So she doesn't eat like that?"

"Some of it might be stuff like that I guess, but she doesn't make it — she has a personal chef to prepare all her food for her."

"And Issy?" asked Kate weakly, recalling the hours of effort she'd put into painstakingly making the meal.

"She just eats normal kids' stuff," admitted Joe. "Genevieve's not happy about that, but I put my foot down about it years ago. The agreement is that she's never photographed eating." He smiled apologetically.

"Oh," said Kate, sinking down into her chair despondently.

"But the food looks great, and I'm starving," said Joe cheerfully.

"It looks like pickled artichoke!" wailed Kate.

"Well . . . yes."

"I can't make the children eat this!" Kate waved vaguely at the result of all her hard work and thought of her wasted afternoon. "What am I going to do?"

Joe came over and knelt next to her, taking her hand. "You are going to pop into town for fish and chips for us all, my treat, and I'll get the kids bathed. You and I can eat all this over the next couple of days."

Kate took a moment, then sighed slowly, letting go of all her stress. There was no harm done. And at the very least she'd have a pretty amusing story to tell Becca when she next saw her. "That sounds like a plan!" she said with a smile.

Joe hugged her, "You are amazing to go to so much trouble for my little girl. I really appreciate it."

"I just wanted her to feel welcome."

"I know you did. And I'm sure she does Kate, you're fantastic."

* * *

Kate was back half an hour later with steaming parcels of fish and chips. The table had been cleared of the other food and Joe had buttered slices of bread and found the vinegar and ketchup. The children were both in their pyjamas and cheerfully tucked into their meal.

Joe leant over to Kate and whispered, "Genevieve would have a fit if she could see this!"

Kate giggled, but quickly collected herself. "I shouldn't be laughing. Genevieve's Issy's mother, I don't want her to be unhappy with anything I'm doing with her daughter."

"Trust me Kate; no one can do anything completely right for Issy according to Genevieve. Issy's staying with me though, and I say it's fine for her to have fish and chips this evening."

"Fair enough," said Kate. She still wasn't entirely comfortable going against Issy's mother's wishes, but Joe was the little girl's father, and surely he also had the right to make decisions for his daughter? And she couldn't deny that Issy was enjoying her meal.

Once they'd finished, the children went out to the garden to play in the last of the daylight, and Kate and Joe cleared up and loaded the dishwasher.

Smiling, Kate watched the two new friends running around together on the lawn. They seemed to be getting on well already; she hoped their friendship continued.

Who knew what would happen with her and Joe, and she shouldn't get ahead of herself, but it was hard at moments like this not to fantasise about the future. Even if it was still almost impossible to imagine she might have a future with someone as ludicrously famous as Joe. Deep down she couldn't help but feel he was so, so far out of her league. And how could she possibly take Genevieve's place? Joe was used to a goddess, and she was just, well, ordinary, simple Kate.

CHAPTER TEN

Issy was a funny little thing, so perfectly turned out, quiet and serious. She didn't look like she was capable of getting really messy or silly. Kate couldn't imagine her ever doing anything naughty, or even just making a tip of her bedroom as her son so often did. And she wasn't the only one unsure of their new guest: Charlie was definitely perplexed by this beautiful creature.

Issy usually went to an exclusive school in LA, unless both Joe and Genevieve had to work away, then she had a private tutor, but Joe hadn't organised for one to start working with her yet. As the Easter holidays were upon them, he figured he could leave sorting that out for a few weeks. The children were happy enough together when Charlie got in from school each day, their games mainly involved Charlie playing like he usually did, but with Issy observing him quietly, following him around like a shadow. Even when the pair watched television together, it was clearly Charlie's choice. Kate had tried asking Issy if she'd rather something else was put on, but she'd just said she was fine. Kate hoped the little girl would be able to relax more soon.

* * *

Early Saturday, a rather harassed looking Joe was at Kate's front door, with Issy in tow.

"My manager's calling me this morning," he explained. "It could go on for a while. Is it alright if I leave Issy with you for a bit?"

"Sure, of course! I'll have her for as long as you need."

"I should be finished by lunchtime."

"Great."

Joe gave Issy a kiss on the top of her head and left.

Inscrutable, huge, blue eyes looked expectantly up at Kate.

"Charlie!" Kate called, needing back-up. Just what was she going to do with Issy for the next few hours?

Her sidekick came racing down the stairs in his usual haphazard way. He wore tracksuit bottoms and a hooded sweatshirt, and hadn't remembered to put any socks on. He made quite a contrast to Issy in her spotless white tights, classic smocked dress, and cardigan.

Only her hair wasn't perfect: it looked rather wayward, giving away the fact that her father wasn't much of a hairstylist.

"Hi Issy!" called Charlie cheerfully. "Mum, is Issy coming to the woods with us?"

Oh damn, thought Kate. She'd forgotten she'd promised to take Charlie to the woods. He'd been looking forward to it as a treat for the first day of the holidays.

"I guess so, sweetie. Is that ok with you, Issy?"

Issy silently nodded.

"Right, Charlie, you get some socks on. Issy, let's get that hair tied back and see if we can find you some wellies."

Kate put Issy's hair in two plaits and unearthed some dinosaur wellington boots Charlie had grown out of which seemed to fit the little girl. She popped Charlie's spare raincoat on her while Charlie himself still forlornly searched around for his socks.

The woods Kate and Charlie had planned to visit weren't too far away: a short drive and they'd be there.

Parking in her usual lay-by, they set off along the bridleway. The weather was overcast but dry, at least for the moment. Usually, Charlie would be running around all over the place by this point, exploring everything. He'd already be covered with the mud caused by the last few days' rain. But now he was walking nicely just ahead of Kate, side by side with Issy. Kate couldn't believe she was actually missing his usual high spirits and busyness, although she had to admit Charlie and Issy looked cute together.

Charlie wittered away to Issy about this and that, how this was his favourite woods and how there was a "huge" stream they'd have to cross.

Going into the woods proper, old hands Kate and Charlie set about collecting small sticks, while Issy, aloof and cautious, looked on. Cajoling, Kate slowly talked her into joining them as they made fairy castles with their bounty. She seemed to enjoy that — it must appeal to her meticulous nature Kate thought as she watched the little girl carefully placing the twigs so they fitted together almost perfectly. Charlie, meanwhile, had long finished his, and was busy investigating an interesting hole by the base of an oak tree.

They moved on and crossed the stream Charlie had warned Issy about; it really was hardly more than a trickle — Charlie marched through it happily, but Kate made sure she held Issy's hand.

Meandering further amongst the trunks and fallen leaves, they followed the uneven, mucky trail. It might be her imagination, but Issy did appear, finally, to be opening up a bit, Kate felt optimistically — of her own accord she'd even joined Charlie in his return to stick finding, his perennial woodland activity.

They began to descend a short incline, the children in the lead. Unfortunately, Kate was so busy watching the kids, that she didn't properly look where she was stepping and lost her footing in the mud. Her legs were out from under her before she even knew what was happening, and she landed hard on her backside, catching poor Charlie and taking him with her on her way down. He grasped at Issy as he slipped, and they all slid together to the bottom of the slope.

The three of them lay prostrate in the mud in silence while they processed just what had happened. Kate looked anxiously at Issy, waiting for the tears to start. Charlie was pretty hardy, and was well used to being covered in dirt, but she didn't think his delicate and previously pristine companion would cope somehow. She began frantically calculating the quickest route to get the little girl back to the house.

The silence was broken by the sound of Issy's laughter. It was swiftly joined by Charlie's infectious giggle and, with relief, Kate's own chortle.

When they'd all stopped laughing enough for them to attempt to move, Kate pulled herself up with a loud squelch. She held out a hand to each of the children and, with a big heave, dragged them both out of the ooze.

Kate was about to declare they'd better make their way home straight away when Issy shouted, "I'm a mud monster!" and the children ran off chasing one another and whooping happily.

Shrugging her shoulders to herself, she set off after them, a big smile on her face.

* * *

When Joe materialised, he found her and the children all curled up on the sofa, hot chocolates in their hands, watching *Toy Story*.

"Hiya! Make yourself a hot chocolate, marshmallows are on the side," said Kate.

"Okay, thanks," replied Joe.

"Hi Daddy!" said Issy, briefly looking away from the screen.

"Hey there rug rat, have you had a good time?"

"The best!" said Issy, before turning back to the film.

They budged up and Joe joined them on the sofa with his drink. It wasn't until the film finished and Issy and

Charlie climbed out from under their blanket, that Joe realised his daughter was wearing Spiderman pyjamas.

Kate saw Joe taking in Issy's outfit.

"We went for a walk in the woods and Issy got a bit muddy," she explained.

"I fell in the mud, Daddy, and it was everywhere!" piped up Issy. "I had to have a bath and Kate washed my hair with strawberry shampoo, AND," she added seriously, "I am wearing boy pants. But they are clean."

"Goodness, it does sound like you've had an adventure!" said Joe.

"Yes. Come on Charlie. Let's go and play dinosaurs!" said Issy, and the children raced up the stairs roaring loudly.

"What on earth have you done to my daughter?" asked Joe laughing.

"I'm really sorry. I hadn't anticipated just how muddy the woods would be. I would have washed Issy's clothes, but the dress said dry-clean only, and the tights looked pretty delicate."

Joe shook his head. "Don't worry about it."

"I'll take them to the dry cleaners tomorrow . . ."

"It doesn't matter."

"But Genevieve . . ."

"Won't notice if they don't return with Issy, honestly." Joe took her hand. "She hasn't even seen the majority of Issy's clothes, her personal assistant will have packed Issy's case, and most of the clothes are donated by designers hoping Issy will be papped wearing them."

"Oh."

"I'm much more interested in hearing about what a fantastic time you guys had. I don't think I've ever seen Issy be noisy, it's great! She's usually so restrained."

Kate relaxed and laughed. If Joe was happy with what had gone on, then it must be alright. And it certainly sounded like the children were having a grand old time upstairs.

"I've been thinking, I could really do with taking Issy to see my mum soon," Joe said the following day. "She hasn't seen either of us for months, and I know she gets lonely living by herself. She's not too far away from here — a couple of hours drive. It's just going to be awkward getting to her, there are bound to be at least a couple of reporters parked outside. Could I borrow your car do you think? To be a bit more inconspicuous?"

"Why don't you invite your mum to stay here?" Kate said. "You've got plenty of room in the barn, she'll have a lovely little break, and get to see her son and granddaughter, and you won't get spotted by any sneaky reporters. It's a win-win."

"Do you know, that might actually be a brilliant idea. I don't think Mum has had a holiday since she came to visit me in LA last year. It'll do her the world of good to have a change of scene, and much less stressful for me than trying to sneak us into her house and getting holed up there if we're spotted." He grinned. "You're a genius."

"Yes, I suppose I am," said Kate laughing.

"I'll call her now and see what she thinks. I'll only be a few minutes," he said, kissing Kate before getting his mobile out. Kate smiled to herself as she listened in. Joe's mum, Diana, was obviously delighted at his suggestion, and it made her feel good that she'd come up with a plan which might sort out the awkward situation.

Joe enveloped her in a big bear hug as soon as he'd hung up.

"Thank you," he said simply. "My mum's absolutely thrilled, and she can't wait to see you again."

"Have you told her about us?" Kate asked, then immediately wished she hadn't in case she sounded needy. Despite her fears, she just liked Joe so much; she had to keep reminding herself of the complexity of their circumstances. What they had was so new, and so fragile. She needed to keep herself in check.

"I have," Joe replied, making Kate's heart swoon. "I told her how awesome you are and how happy you make me."

Kate was embarrassed by Joe's declaration, as lovely as it was, so turned away to get some cutlery from the drawer.

119

Misinterpreting her reaction, he asked, "It's okay I told her, isn't it?"

"Of course! I just wasn't sure if you would."

"She's coming tomorrow — if that's alright? She was so pleased."

"Great, I'll get the fold-out bed made up for her."

"I can do that," said Joe. "I don't like you running around after me."

"You must be used to people running around after you!"

"Other people, yes," Joe admitted, slightly sheepishly. "But not you, Kate."

"I'll find the sheets and you can do it yourself then."

"Thanks."

"I wonder how much *Hello!* magazine would pay for photos of you changing a bed?" Kate joked, pulling out her phone playfully.

"Oh, probably millions. But I'll make sure I wear my baseball cap and shades so you'll never be able to prove it was me."

"Damn, all my dreams of fame and fortune, destroyed."

"Probably not a bad thing," he said sadly, suddenly sombre, all trace of the light-hearted banter gone. "Fame and fortune really aren't all they're cut out to be."

CHAPTER ELEVEN

It was sweet to see Joe so unsure of himself before his mother arrived. He proclaimed at breakfast the following morning that he was going to clean the barn, something he hadn't let Kate do much during his stay as he hated the thought of her tidying up after him. Kate immediately offered to help at least, if not do the entire job herself as he was technically her customer, but he refused her assistance, only accepting the cleaning products she produced. He took hold of them gamely, though she suspected he didn't have much idea what most of them did. He and Issy went off back down the path determinedly, her waving a large pink feather duster in the air.

An hour later, a hot and bothered looking Joe returned to Kate's house to ask if she could watch Issy for him for a while. It seemed the little girl wasn't quite as much help as he'd thought she'd be.

Charlie and Issy followed Kate around as she took care of her own jobs. They were putting some strawberry plants in one of the new raised beds, when a van drove along the track at the end of the garden. Kate could make out the words "Spick and Span Cleaners" on the side through gaps in the hedge. Oh dear! Joe must have worked himself into quite a state to resort to calling in an emergency cleaning company!

The children went to make a fort in the sitting room while Kate had some phone calls and paperwork to take care of. By then it was time for lunch. Kate texted Joe to see if he wanted to eat with them, but he replied quickly saying he was still busy so would sort himself out with something. He'd see them as soon as he was done.

After eating in the fort, Charlie and Issy decided to play Lego in Charlie's bedroom.

Eventually, Kate heard the company's van driving back past and a few minutes later, Joe was at the door returning her cleaning supplies.

"Sorry I've been a while," he said. "It took longer than I'd anticipated."

"Oh yeah?" said Kate, biting her lip to refrain from grinning. "You gave the place a really good going over, did you?"

"Well, yeah. I want it to look it's best for when my mum arrives later," Joe said, looking shamefaced. Kate glared at him mock-sternly. "Joe . . ."

"You know I paid someone to come and do the cleaning, don't you?"

"I spotted the van through the hedge as it went past."

"Turns out I'm pretty rubbish at housework. Oh, and I'll replace the lampshade, just tell me where you got it from."

"I'm not even going to ask how that happened."

"It's probably best you don't."

"You do realise you could have just let me help you?"

"I don't want you tidying up after me."

"I don't particularly want to tidy up after you either, but I would have been happy to help out, and it might have saved the lampshade."

"I suppose so," agreed Joe grudgingly.

"Helping each other out when they need it is kind of what couples do. I want the barn to look nice for your mum as well. How about I pop out in a bit to get some fresh flowers for her room and anything else you think she'd like?"

"Thanks, Kate, that's really kind. It's frustrating not being able to go myself to get things like that."

"Well, I don't think it's a great idea for you to come with me to the supermarket in case you're spotted, but I can call you from there and talk you through what they've got?"

"That would be great," Joe replied.

"Actually, weren't you worried about the cleaning lady recognising you? Or did you make her sign an iron-clad confidentiality agreement before she started?"

"I don't carry a bunch of legal documents around with me to hand out to random cleaning ladies you know!"

"So what did you do? Wear a hat and sunglasses in the house and hope for the best?"

"If you must know . . . I hid," said Joe, with as much dignity as he could muster.

"You hid?!"

"Yes, in my bedroom. It was the only room I'd managed to sort out by myself anyway. I left the money on the dining room table with a note explaining I was ill in bed and wasn't to be disturbed."

"The poor woman must have thought you were bonkers calling her up and then too ill to get out of bed just an hour later!"

"Probably."

"At least the barn is definitely fit for your mum to arrive. Do you know what time she'll be here?"

"About five. She was picked up a while ago by my driver, Mike."

"I thought you and Issy would probably want her to yourselves tonight, so shall I pick you all up a few things for supper when I go to the supermarket?"

"Thanks, that would be great."

She paused. "I needed to speak to you about something, too. I've just had a call from a family wanting to stay in the other barn. It's very short notice — they've been before and only need it for one night but they want to come tomorrow, so I need to get back to them right away . . . to be honest, it would be handy for me to be able to take the booking, I could sort of do with the money," Kate admitted. Normally, she'd have been advertising the holiday lets and the campsite this time of year and would have started to be quite busy, but enjoying the company of her secretive, very special guest, she'd been holding off promoting or taking reservations for as long as she could.

"I'm happy to pay more," said Joe immediately. "I'll pay for both the barns; it's really not a problem."

"That's very generous of you, but I wouldn't want that, I'd feel uncomfortable."

"I understand, and of course, book them in. I'll just stay out of their way."

"It shouldn't be too much of a pain because of the separate driveways leading up from here, and they can't see your barn from theirs. The only time you'd bump into each other is if you were both coming to this house at the same time — but from what they said on the phone, they're staying for a family thing and will only really be using the barn to sleep."

"I'm sure it'll be fine."

"They wanted to check in at about midday tomorrow. Why don't you bring your mum here for lunch at half one? They should be unpacked and well out of the way by then."

* * *

The arrival of her new guests was a very welcome distraction for Kate the next morning. She put the finishing touches to Cherry Barn — ensuring there was fresh linen and towels and putting a few essentials in the kitchen, along with some extras they'd asked her to get in for them. All the busyness helped take her mind off seeing Diana later; it was silly, but she'd woken feeling anxious, like a teenager again, nervous at meeting her boyfriend's parents for the first time. She kept trying to reassure herself that Diana would no doubt be terribly grateful Joe's new girlfriend was far more normal and down to earth than his soon-to-be-ex-wife. And, as she was divorced herself, Kate was fairly sure she wouldn't be pushing Joe back towards the "sanctity" of his unhappy marriage, so at least Kate didn't have that to worry about.

She'd met Diana several times already when she and Joe were teenagers. Diana had always been welcoming, but reserved: quiet and perhaps a little sad. She was dealing with her husband leaving her only a few months before they moved, and, naturally, worrying about her son who must have been missing his father dreadfully. Not that Joe ever talked about it much at the time.

As an old school friend of his, Kate felt she must have something going for her, but Diana was bound to have concerns at the speed things were moving, about her son entering into another relationship this soon — especially as his last was only now publicly falling apart. And certainly concerned about the effect of everything on her granddaughter. Aside from all that, there was also the very considerable wealth difference: maybe Diana would even see her as a gold digger, out to entrap her vulnerable boy!

Kate took a deep breath and consciously pulled herself together. Worrying like this wasn't going to help anything.

She'd seen Joe's car go past her house the previous afternoon but hadn't been able to catch a glimpse of his mother. She tried to visualise Diana in her mind, but it wasn't easy, it had been such a long time.

The Cherry Barn family had arrived on time and Kate quickly settled them in. They were going out later that afternoon she discovered, but were planning to relax in the barn for a few hours first. The weather was miserable so they weren't likely to go for a walk. Joe, Issy and his mum should still be fine to slip down to her house for lunch.

Kate had made a lasagne from scratch the night before in preparation and was putting it in the oven to heat through when the telephone rang. She picked it up, expecting it was Joe calling to check the coast was clear for them to come round, but a female voice greeted her.

"Hi, I was hoping to make a reservation for one of your holiday homes," said the woman.

"Of course, only the larger barn is available though, I'm afraid."

"Either is fine."

"When did you want to come?"

"As soon as possible please."

"Both barns are occupied at the moment, but the larger one will be free from mid-afternoon tomorrow."

"So the other barn will still have its guest in then?" asked the woman, rather quickly.

"Yes, is that a problem?"

"No, not at all, the larger barn would be brilliant."

"How long would you like to stay?" Kate asked, pleased to be taking bookings again, though still determined not to take in any campers. Having her usual number of Easter holidaymakers around really would be pushing Joe's luck in not being recognised.

"I'll arrive Thursday morning and stay until Saturday please."

"And how many people will be staying?"

"Just me."

"Oh. It's rather a large house for one person."

"That's fine," said the woman. "I like to have space."

"Alright," said Kate. She'd never had just a single occupant in Cherry Barn before. The current rates were lower than in the summer, so it wasn't quite as expensive as it could be, but it was still pretty pricey for someone on their own. Kate did wonder whether she ought to ask Joe to move into the larger barn so this woman could have the smaller one, but she seemed happy with what was being offered, while Joe had made himself at home with all his music equipment now and it would be awkward getting him to move with Issy and Diana both there as well. His mum had only just arrived; it would be a bit embarrassing to have to explain to her she needed to change where she was staying after only a couple of nights.

Kate took the woman's name and details and said she looked forward to seeing her on Thursday.

She put down the phone feeling pleased. It was nice to have the barns occupied, and Joe would be fine with it, she knew, they'd just have to be careful. Of course, this again brought the fact that she still had absolutely no idea how long Joe was going to be around for to the fore of her mind, but she firmly pushed it out of the way: for the time being at least, she was enjoying what they had while they had it, who knew yet what the future held for them?

When Joe, Issy and Diana arrived, Charlie was introduced and said hello to Diana before he and Issy ran upstairs to no doubt get up to some sort of mischief.

"I remember you coming to my house like it were yesterday," said Diana with a warm, kind smile. She drew Kate into a hug. "You were such a pretty, polite girl, I always thought you and Joe would be good together."

Joe coughed awkwardly. "Mum!" he mumbled.

"Oh hush; it's a mother's prerogative to embarrass her son from time to time. Grown-up or not. I don't get to do it nearly enough, so allow me to now!"

Kate and Joe laughed, and Kate felt the knot of tension in her stomach dissolve.

Diana had obviously aged in the seventeen years since Kate had last seen her, she was almost seventy and her hair was completely grey, but she looked far happier and at ease now. It was very clear she missed and adored Joe from the way she kept constantly looking at him, as if trying to take in as much as him as she possibly could. Kate could more than understand: she was the same with Charlie when he went away for just a couple of nights with his dad. It must be hard for Diana, Kate thought, not seeing her son for months and months at a time, and then only flying visits.

Kate made everyone a cup of tea, and they sat down to chat at the kitchen table, reminiscing about when Joe and Kate were teenagers, and enjoying the sounds filtering down from Charlie's bedroom of the children playing together.

"You have a lovely home," Diana commented to Kate.

"Thank you, Charlie and I are very lucky."

"Does Charlie's father live nearby?"

"Yes, he's still close. He sees lots of Charlie."

"That's good. I think what hurt me the most when Joe's father left was that he didn't keep in touch with Joe."

"Mum, let's not talk about that now," said Joe gently.

"Okay, love. But can I just say how pleased I am that you're still such a large part of Issy's life?"

"I'd never abandon Issy, Mum, you know that," Joe replied.

"Yes, but sometimes these things can get rather complicated. I'm glad you and Genevieve seem to have got things sorted out regarding Issy. Anything else you have to divide up is just stuff after all."

Joe caught Kate's eye. It seemed he hadn't told his mother the trouble he'd been having with his estranged wife and getting access to his daughter.

"Well, nothing formal has been set down between us about Issy, but Genevieve seems happy for me to have her whenever possible," Joe said, diplomatically.

"What about when she goes back to America? I assume that's where she still wants to be based?" Diana asked. "I mean if you're going to be here more," she continued, glancing at Kate.

"We'll sort things out. Genevieve's going to be filming in France for a while yet. If she wants, I'll take Issy over there to visit for a few days, and maybe we'll chat then about where we're both going to live."

"So you haven't talked about anything more long term?" Diana asked.

"No," said Joe. He sighed. "Genevieve's refusing to discuss any of the divorce details, including custody of Issy, until after the film's wrapped."

Kate's unintentional raising of her eyebrows gave away her feelings about this arrangement perfectly, and it seemed Joe's mother agreed with her. "Don't let her boss you around Joe. Issy's just as much your child as she is hers."

"I know, and I don't plan on letting her walk all over me by any means. I'm just hoping if I wait like she wants, she might be more prepared to be reasonable when it comes to hammering out the finer details."

"Do you think she'll cause trouble?" asked Kate, wishing she could stop herself from blurting it out, especially with Diana sitting next to her, but unable to.

"I hope not. But to be honest, it largely depends on what sort of mood she and her obnoxious solicitor are in when we get round to discussing things. But Mum's right: as long as I get proper access to Issy, that's all that really matters."

* * *

Joe came back round to see Kate after Issy had gone to bed that evening. Diana had offered to keep an eye on her, knowing that after the afternoon's conversation her son and his girlfriend would need to chat.

"Hey," said Kate, with a small smile when Joe let himself in and found her answering some emails at her desk. "I didn't expect to see you again today. Is everything alright?"

"Everything's fine. We just hadn't had a chance to be just the two of us today, and I felt like I needed to see you. So I took advantage of having someone to keep an ear out in case Issy needs anything. Is Charlie asleep?"

"Yep. Come on through," she said, getting up. "Would you like a drink?"

"A cup of tea would be great."

Silence hung over the pair as the kettle boiled. Kate had struggled to stop herself from going over and over the implications of what Joe had said earlier but didn't know how to bring the topic up. Was there even really any point in discussing it? Joe didn't know anything for sure, and wouldn't for a while she guessed. It did seem important though that something was said to acknowledge the enormous power Genevieve apparently had over their fledgling relationship. Kate was trying to form the words to bring up the subject, when Joe saved her the trouble, "That conversation with my mum earlier, about Issy, it got me thinking about things I've been trying really, really hard not to think about."

"Yes, me too," said Kate, smiling sadly.

"Issy is the single most important thing in my life . . ." began Joe.

"As she should be," Kate said quietly. "And as Charlie is to me."

"Genevieve may not be the best mother in the world, but she is Issy's mother, and the courts still favour the mother in the majority of custody cases. Anyway, I wouldn't want Issy to have to see her parents fighting over her."

"That's understandable."

"What I'm trying to say is that, if Genevieve demands full custody and decides she wants to continue having Los Angeles as her base, that's where I'm going to have to be. I can't only see Issy a couple of times a year when either she or I can fly over to each other in the school holidays. It's not the sort of father I am."

"I know."

"I suppose what I'm wanting to know, what I'm sounding you out about, is that if Issy is going to be living in America, would you and Charlie consider moving there with me, so we could still be together?"

The look of surprise on Kate's face made Joe backtrack slightly. "Not that I'd expect you to make a definite decision now. I mean it might not even happen, and it's not like we've been together long at all. I am aware of that. I swear I'm not going completely crazy."

Kate took a moment to collect her thoughts. As strong as her feelings were for him, Joe's question had caught her off guard.

"Oh Joe, it's so lovely you'd ask me. If it were just about Charlie and me, I'd say yes in a heartbeat, I'd go with you tomorrow," she said, determined to be as honest as she could be. "But I couldn't do that to Charlie's dad. I couldn't take Charlie away from him like that. Then I'd be behaving just as terribly as Genevieve. Worse even, Nick doesn't have the money to be flying over the Atlantic whenever he felt like it to visit. And there's my mum to think about. She worships Charlie."

"Of course. Of course, you're right," said Joe softly, taking her in his arms. "But what are we going to do?"

"I honestly don't know," Kate replied desolately.

* * *

Kate was tidying away after lunch the next day and wondering what to do with Charlie for the rest of the rather black cloud-covered afternoon when she heard a knock on the door. Answering it, she found Diana and Issy on her doorstep.

"Oh hello!" said Kate cheerfully. "Charlie's upstairs in his room if you'd like to go up and see him," she said to Issy, who immediately made for the stairs, racing up them two at a time. "Would you like a cup of tea?" she asked Diana.

"A quick one would be lovely, if you're not too busy," Joe's mum replied, following Kate into the kitchen. "Joe's catching up on some sleep. I think he was up most of the night composing on his guitar and keyboard."

"Didn't that keep you awake?" asked Kate, filling up the kettle and putting it on to boil.

"Oh no, he's got headphones. I didn't hear a peep."

"That's good," replied Kate, though at that precise moment she could think of nothing nicer than lying in bed listening to Joe playing his guitar.

"Joe does keep some rather peculiar hours," Diana commented. "Although from what I hear, that sort of goes with the job."

"Yes, I imagine it does."

"I expect you're used to more regular timekeeping, with having a little boy and all."

"Well, yes, but Joe's got Issy, I'm sure he's used to getting up early with a child."

"Issy's had nannies since the day she was born. In fact, I remember she had two of them for her first year, one for the day and one for the night. It's hardly the same as being a single mother without that sort of support."

"My mum helps me out a lot," said Kate, becoming a little defensive despite her best intentions. "And Charlie's dad is very much still in the picture."

"I didn't mean to offend you," said Diana quickly. "It's just you and Joe are such complete opposites in so many ways, and I don't think the pair of you are quite aware of that yet. I love my son very, very much, but the life he's chosen to lead is rather unusual, and not at all conducive to family life, at least not from what I can see."

Embarrassed at having such an intimate subject brought up by Joe's mother, Kate replied, "Well, Joe and I are in quite the early stages . . . we'll just take things as they come." Though, since their discussion the previous evening, this was of course no longer strictly true she realised, feeling bad for telling a white lie to Joe's mother.

"I see the two of you, and whether or not you've talked about your future, it's clear what both of you want. I think you make a wonderful couple, but you need to get a few things sorted out if this romance is going to go any further. Before someone gets hurt." Sensing by the look on Kate's face that she'd said enough, at least for now, Diana added, "I thought I'd take the children out, if I may."

"That would be lovely, but you really don't need to take Charlie as well."

"I'd like to. He's a charming little boy, and a great friend to my granddaughter."

"Well . . . it's very kind of you. Where were you planning to take them?"

"If Joe's driver is able to take us, I thought they might like to go to the pictures, there's some new dinosaur movie Issy fancies on at the cinema in town, and then I'll cook them some tea. Joe says it's fine as long as I get Issy inside the cinema quickly. She won't be recognised without him with her."

"They'll love that, and the cinema in town is always really quiet mid-afternoon. Why don't you borrow my car though?"

"Oh, could I? That would be wonderful, thank you," said Diana appreciatively.

* * *

Alone with her thoughts, Kate went over what Diana had said. She shouldn't feel hurt by it she supposed. Diana wanted the best for them. And she was probably right: she knew so little about Joe's "usual" life, but what she did know made her suspect she wouldn't fit into it very well.

She couldn't imagine herself attending an endless line of premieres or following Joe around the world while he toured. Perhaps that sort of existence would be fun for a while, but not permanently. And what about Charlie's education? He loved the small, local school he went to. From the little she knew of the children of the super-rich and famous, they either followed their parents around, flitting about and making it hard to put down roots and forge lasting friendships, or they went to boarding school. Neither sounded much like an option she'd be happy with for Charlie.

But, despite these fears, and what Diana had said, Kate didn't feel she could speak to Joe about them: he had enough to worry about making sure he had proper access to Issy, and that had to be his priority. She resolved not to say anything of her worries to him. They should just enjoy what they have and see where it developed. And if it was all over in a couple of weeks, well, she'd have some amazing memories.

CHAPTER TWELVE

Kate stretched in bed, rumpling the duvet but smoothing out the stiffness of her interrupted sleep. Seeing the sun shining, albeit somewhat weakly, through her bedroom window lifted her tired and troubled spirits, and when Charlie came bouncing energetically in a little later, she couldn't help smiling. Nothing she could do would make the slightest bit of difference to what the future held for her and Joe, but it would spoil the beautiful day if she allowed herself to be in a bad mood about it.

She and Charlie went downstairs for breakfast and Kate saw she had a text message on her mobile from Joe checking she was alright. She called him back while she made her morning cuppa and poured Charlie some cornflakes.

"Hey," he answered. "What are you up to?"

"Having some breakfast before the woman who's booked Cherry Barn arrives. Have you got any plans for today?"

"No, not really. Just spending time with Mum and Issy. It's Mum's last day here, she needs to get back to her cats. My driver's going to take her home in the evening so I was thinking, if you're free, we could all risk going out for a few hours today. Take the kids to the seaside with their buckets and spades? It's not going to be exactly paddling weather, but it's supposed to be dry and bright."

"I'm free! And I know a beach that won't be busy, with a café to get some ice creams from. It should be open, and they have some tables round the back; no one will spot you there."

"Great." She could sense Joe smiling at the other end of the line. "Have you got a hat Issy could borrow?"

"Sure. If I pop her in some of Charlie's jeans and a sweatshirt, and tie her hair up, no one will recognise her."

"Great. You're wonderful! I'll go tell Mum."

As the phone call ended, a small silver BMW pulled up outside the house, Kate went to greet her guest, a short, slim young woman with shoulder-length black hair and a beak-like nose.

"Hello," said the woman, extending her hand to Kate. "I'm Julia, I've booked one of your barns, we spoke on the phone." Her frozen, wax-like smile hung a second too long, then disappeared as abruptly as it had come.

"Of course. Let me grab the keys and I'll meet you there, just follow the track around to the right."

* * *

Julia was waiting by the door of the barn when Kate arrived.

"Lovely spot here!" she commented. "Have you got other guests staying at the moment?"

"The other barn's being used, as I said before," replied Kate. "But I'm not booking campers into the field at the moment, it needs some work doing to it."

"It's very private here, isn't it?"

"That's part of the charm."

"I'm sure the other barn's lovely as well. How lucky for someone to be able to have a long stay there! I imagine you know when they'll be leaving though."

"Not exactly," Kate said lightly.

This woman was really nosy, and there was an air about her that made Kate's skin crawl. She just wanted to be done with her, finish getting ready and go out, so she said, "Hopefully you'll have everything you need here, but if you

135

have any problems, give me a call. The number's on the side in the kitchen and in the welcome folder," and then made as swift an exit as she could.

* * *

Julia managed a full quarter of an hour by herself before Kate heard a voice calling, "Hellooooooo!" from the front door. "It's Julia!"

"Come on in," replied Kate, as sweetly as she could manage. She didn't entirely know why, but she'd taken an immediate dislike to the new guest. She suspected it wasn't completely to do with the woman herself, more to do with her being worried Julia would bump into Joe. Though there was undoubtedly something in the woman's manner that didn't sit quite right.

Julia joined her in the kitchen. "What a lovely home you have!" she exclaimed, looking around and seeming to photograph everything with her eyes. She made Kate feel uncomfortable, as if she and her house were being scrutinised and catalogued.

"Thank you," Kate said, as cheerfully as she could muster. "How can I help? Is everything alright with the barn?"

"Oh yes, it's wonderful," gushed Julia, still glancing around her. "I was just wondering if I could have the Wi-Fi code?"

"It's in the folder on the coffee table in your sitting room," Kate answered.

"Silly me," said Julia, "I didn't think to look there . . ."

"Don't worry, I'll write it down for you anyway," said Kate, going to her desk for a pen and paper.

"Do you live alone?" enquired Julia pryingly.

"With my son," said Kate, handing Julia the code.

"No man on the scene then?"

"Nope," replied Kate shortly, really wishing the other woman would mind her own business.

Julia looked as if she was about to start another line of questioning, but Kate said, "I'm ever so sorry I don't have time to chat, but we're just on our way out."

"Anywhere nice?"

"The seaside. Now, if there isn't anything else . . ." Kate held the front door open.

"Is it a local beach you're going to?"

"Fairly," Kate said, cagily. The guest's inquisitiveness was definitely getting on her nerves.

"I'll let you get on then, thank you," said Julia, finally getting the hint and leaving.

Kate waited a minute, to ensure Julia was well out of the way, and texted Joe to tell him the coast was clear.

He arrived soon after with Issy and Diana. Five minutes later, Issy looked nothing like her usual self: dressed in Charlie's clothes, with her hair tied up and tucked inside a cap, she could easily have passed for a little boy. She wasn't at all bothered by her unusual appearance but was ecstatic at the thought of going to the seaside with her friend.

They all piled into Kate's car; along with what seemed like enough stuff for at least a week's holiday packed in around them. Joe was squashed in the back between the children so his mum could be comfortable in the front.

He really was so relaxed and easy-going, chatting away to the little ones and playing car games with them, that it was hard to remember just how very different his life usually was to this. It gave Kate hope that maybe there was some way they could carry on their relationship after this bubble of alternative reality popped.

The only other people on the beach were a few dog walkers, who didn't give the group a second look. It was still a bit chilly for most families to venture down there.

The day was bright, but cold. They were all glad of their coats as they pottered along, enjoying the antics of the swooping seagulls. The children happily entertained themselves, clambering over boulders and poking about in rock pools. They delighted in bossing the grown-ups around when everyone built an enormous sandcastle together.

The café was deserted when they trundled up to it, so they decided to risk sitting inside by the window so they could warm up a bit next to a radiator. The view of the sea was gorgeous. Joe and Issy kept their caps on and sat with their backs to the counter in case they were recognised by the chatty owner. They all enjoyed bacon sandwiches made with thick, soft white bread followed by coffee for the adults and ice cream for the children.

They went for a walk along the cliff top after lunch, the children running here, there and everywhere.

Eventually, they got back to the car, and within five minutes, both Charlie and Issy were fast asleep. Of course, having rested, once home the children were full of beans again while everyone else was dying to put their feet up and relax.

Diana left them to go and finish her packing, and have half an hour's peace with a cup of tea before Joe's driver came to pick her up.

Joe and Issy walked over to the barn to say goodbye when they saw the car pass, but Kate and Charlie stayed. She didn't want to intrude on the family farewell. It wasn't long, however, before she heard the car stop outside, and Kate went to wish Joe's mum a safe journey. Diana was getting out and came over to Kate and wrapped her in a hug.

"Thank you. For everything," she said hoarsely.

"It was no trouble at all, it's been a pleasure having you here," said Kate.

"No, not just for the last few days. For everything you've done for Joe. I feel like I have my son back. You obviously make him happy."

She gave a little sniff as she stepped away, full of checked emotion. Bending down, she said farewell to Charlie, "And thank you for being such a good friend to my granddaughter, she's a very lucky girl."

"No problem," said Charlie seriously and he shook Diana's proffered hand.

With a final smile, Joe's mother got back in the car and it drove off.

* * *

"Guess what? That Julia woman has gone! She must have left late last night; the keys were just posted through the letter box. I guess she can't have liked the place, but she didn't say anything was wrong," exclaimed Kate the following morning when Joe wandered into the kitchen to find her and coffee.

"Maybe she just had to get back to work early or something, I'm sure it wasn't the barn," Joe said, coming over to give her a kiss.

"You look very pleased with yourself," Kate commented.

"I've got a lot to be happy about," he said genially. "A beautiful woman, my daughter with me, and the songs are really coming together for the new album. I was worried that perhaps I couldn't do it anymore, that maybe all the music I had to write I'd done. But I guess not."

"That's brilliant," said Kate, touching his arm, "I can't wait to hear them properly."

"I'm a bit nervous about that, some of them are about you."

"Really?"

"Yep."

"I'm not sure I'm really interesting enough to write songs about," said Kate laughing.

"I'm sure you are," replied Joe, pulling her in for another kiss. "Also," he continued, "I've got a great plan for today: why don't we take the kids out sailing? It's perfect weather for it and I haven't been able to get Issy on the water for ages. We could make some sandwiches and then pick up some chips on the way home."

"We wouldn't all fit on your friend's boat though, would we? It'd be a bit of a squeeze, and I'd be worried about Charlie. He's never been sailing before, and he's not the strongest of swimmers . . ."

"Um . . ." Joe hesitated, looking slightly abashed. "He's got a bigger boat we can use. It'll be perfectly safe I promise. I'll need to pick up a buoyancy aid for Charlie though, I've only got one little one. There's a shop not too far from here. If you're happy to look after Issy for a while, and I can borrow your car, I'll go and pick one up."

"What if someone spots you?"

"I'll wear my baseball cap and I'll only be in the shop for a few minutes." He grinned. "I'm feeling reckless today!"

"Okay . . . if you're sure."

"I am. You wouldn't know what to get if you went by yourself, and if we all go we'll only have to make the packed lunches when we come back. This way, I'm hoping all the hard work will have been done while I'm out!" said Joe cheekily.

"Makes sense," said Kate. "And of course you can borrow the car, the keys are in the pot on the hall table, and Issy's no trouble. They'll probably just watch some cartoons while I get stuff ready."

"Remember sun cream," advised Joe. "I know it's not hot, but the sun's out and when it's reflecting off the water it's easy to get burnt."

"Aye aye captain!"

"See you in a bit then."

Joe left and, as expected, the two children soon came thundering down the stairs to ask if they could watch a DVD. Kate put *The Lego Movie* on for them and then went back into the kitchen to begin making the picnic.

She'd finished the sandwiches and was scavenging in the cupboards for crisps and granola bars, when she heard a knock on the door. Assuming it was Joe back already and he'd forgotten his key, she called out to Charlie to let him in.

"Ms Holloway?" said the clipped tones of a Home Counties accent moments later. Kate turned and was faced with a tall, very skinny, young woman with poker straight, long, blond hair. She wore heavy eye make-up and a stark white shirt with a short grey skirt and matching suit jacket. The overall impression was Office Barbie.

"Yes, I'm Ms Holloway," Kate replied, "How can I help you?"

"My name's Arabella. I'm Genevieve Moore's personal assistant." Two hard-faced men in suits framed the doorway behind her.

"Oh, right," said Kate, subtly trying to tidy herself up a bit, she felt a terrible mess next to this flawless, epitome of efficiency, and at a disadvantage.

"I'm looking for Joseph Wild. I tried the address he's given but no one was in, so Genevieve suggested I try here."

"Joe's not about at the moment. He's gone out, but he shouldn't be long. Can I help?" asked Kate, trying to be as pleasant as possible.

"I wouldn't have thought so," said Arabella snootily. "Genevieve has sent me to pick up Ismene. She wishes her daughter to join her in France immediately."

"But Issy, Ismene, is staying with her father at the moment, until Genevieve finishes filming," Kate explained. "That's what they'd agreed upon."

"Well I'm sure you'll concur with Genevieve that the situation has changed somewhat since that agreement was reached."

By way of explanation, Arabella marched past Kate, put her briefcase on the table, opened it and took out a pile of newspapers. Fanning them out over the surface, she said, "You can keep these."

Kate picked up the paper closest to her. Plastered across the front page was a photo of her, Joe and Issy eating their ice creams at the café. Charlie and Diana weren't in the picture. They'd been on the other side of the table and the photographer probably hadn't thought them interesting enough to take a shot of. The headline accompanying the story screamed, "New Love for Wild". Kate could feel Arabella watching her as she quickly skimmed the article. It didn't name Kate but detailed the whole of the outing. It pointed out how happy Kate and Joe looked together, and how relaxed Issy seemed around Kate. Then the obvious suggestion was made that

141

Joe had left Genevieve for this new woman. Apparently "Ms Moore was unavailable for comment" but a "close friend" was quoted as saying Genevieve was "distraught".

"But most of this is absolute rubbish!" exclaimed Kate stunned.

"Even so. They haven't named you yet, but it won't be long. I'm amazed you haven't got reporters camped out on your doorstep already," retorted Arabella. "I'm sure you'll agree it's in Ismene's best interests to get her out of here, and back to her mother, as soon as possible."

Kate tried to think quickly. She couldn't deny it was likely the house would be under siege very shortly, but it wasn't up to her to make any decision about Issy, she wasn't her parent.

Issy and Charlie took that moment to decide to join the grown-ups in the kitchen.

"Ah, Ismene," said Arabella brightly, catching sight of her prey. "Just the girl I've been looking for."

Ismene looked absolutely petrified, turning to Kate for support. But before Kate could say anything to reassure the child, Arabella said, "Ismene I've come to take you to stay with your mother."

"But Issy's playing with me," blurted out Charlie innocently. "We were going to get my bike out."

"Well I'm afraid that just won't be possible," replied Arabella.

"I want to play on the bike," said Issy quietly.

"Maybe your mother will buy you a bike," Arabella said sharply. "But we need to leave now."

"I'll call Joe first," said Kate. "Honestly; he should be back any moment."

"I'm sure you understand why we must go straight away."

"You can't take her without checking with her father! And what about Issy's things? They're in the barn you knocked at."

"Ismene has plenty of 'things' with Genevieve," said Arabella, picking up her briefcase. "Ismene get your shoes please. We're going."

Kate grabbed her mobile phone and quickly dialled Joe's number. The sound of ringing came from under some junk mail on the kitchen counter. Joe had obviously left his phone behind.

"Genevieve Moore for you," said Arabella, pushing her own mobile into Kate's hands.

"Hello," said Kate.

The unmistakable drawl of Joe's estranged wife replied, "Arabella is collecting my daughter now. You hand her over, or I'm sending my lawyer."

The phone line went dead.

Poor Issy looked close to tears, and Kate didn't know what she should do. Her gut told her she should refuse to allow Arabella to take Issy before Joe returned, but how could she stop her with her mother demanding it? As if sensing Kate was plotting mutiny, Arabella hissed quietly to her, "Do you really want her to leave upset?"

Arabella's silent companions loomed closer, a menacing threat of the inevitable.

Kate stopped herself. Of course she didn't want Issy to be dragged off kicking and screaming. She just wished Joe would come through the door and take over. Charlie clung to her, something he hadn't done for a long time. He was obviously worried about the situation, didn't understand what was going on, and didn't like the atmosphere which hung over the kitchen like a heavy fog.

Issy hadn't moved, but looked as if she were debating joining Charlie with his mother for some sort of comfort.

"Ismene, get your shoes please," Arabella repeated, more irritably.

Issy turned and walked out into the hallway. Kate shot a glare at Arabella and followed the little girl. She felt terrible, like she was betraying Issy and the trust Joe had placed in her to look after his daughter. She helped Issy on with her shoes and found her coat. She noticed Charlie run upstairs and wanted to follow him, to check he was alright, but she needed to be with Issy at the moment. Kate stared at the front door as Issy got ready, willing it, with every fibre of her being, to open and for Joe to be standing there.

She thought furiously: there had to be a way of stopping this, there had to be. Could she call the police? But what could they do? The two thugs would simply take the girl and be long gone before anyone arrived — that would be awful for Issy. It would solve nothing and the fallout for Joe with his divorce if it got to the press, would make everything much, much worse. Damn it! She was basically helpless.

Charlie came racing down the stairs again. He went straight to his friend and gave her a slightly awkward hug. He handed her something. "It's my best one," Kate heard him whisper. "I want you to have it." Issy said nothing but took her gift and held it tightly in her fist.

Arabella stood impatiently, tapping her foot, as Kate helped Issy on with her coat and kissed her forehead. "I'm sure we'll see you very soon," she said to the little girl.

"Don't count on it," she heard Arabella murmur behind her scornfully.

Arabella seemed to think she was in danger of losing control of the situation as emotions were beginning to run high. She nudged past Kate, a little more roughly than was perhaps strictly necessary, and took Issy's hand.

"Goodbye," she said, before turning and letting herself out of the front door. Kate and Charlie followed behind and watched as the driver of the huge Bentley Arabella had arrived in got out of his seat and lifted Issy into the back of the car. The two minders flanked her on either side. Arabella herself slid into the front passenger seat and within seconds the car was speeding down the driveway in a cloud of dust. Issy waved to Kate and Charlie through the back window for at least as long as they could see her. Kate's eyes filled with tears, but she knew she had to hold herself together for Charlie and Joe. Oh God, what was Joe going to say when he found out what had happened? Would he blame her? She didn't have long to find out because as she and Charlie were turning to return inside, Joe's car pulled in.

He got out holding up the newly purchased buoyancy aid triumphantly, but instantly realised all was not well.

"What's the matter?" he asked, walking towards them anxiously. A pregnant silence formed as she struggled to marshal herself. "Where's Issy?" he followed, with increasing alarm, seeing she wasn't with them.

"Oh Joe, I'm so sorry," Kate began, "Come inside."

"Is she hurt?" Joe said, sounding terrified and seemingly rooted to the spot.

"No, she's not hurt," Kate answered immediately. "But Genevieve sent her assistant, some horrible woman called Arabella to pick her up."

"Pick her up? Why? Where is she taking her? Is Genevieve in the UK?"

"I don't know — I think Genevieve's still in France. She's decided she wants Issy with her."

"But she can't do that!" Joe said loudly, making Charlie jump. "Why did you let Arabella take Issy? Why couldn't she wait until I was back or at least call me to let me know what she wanted? She can't just whisk my daughter away and take her to another country without even informing me. How could you?"

"There wasn't anything I could do! You left your mobile here, so I wasn't able to call you," explained Kate, trying to keep as calm as possible and not let Joe's harsh words hurt her. He was upset, it was natural he'd lash out.

"But why has she done this?" said Joe desperately.

She sighed. "Come inside and I'll show you."

Charlie continued holding onto Kate as they went inside the house, looking from her to Joe and back again, trying to work out what was going on. Kate squeezed his hand gently, hoping to convey some form of reassurance.

Kate pointed to the newspapers still strewn out on the kitchen table. Joe quickly scanned them, the worry on his face again rapidly turning to anger. He picked up the tabloidiest of the bunch, his brow furrowing more the further he read. He was silent, and Kate stood apprehensively waiting for his response.

"I need to call Genevieve," he said distractedly. He put down the paper and, locating his mobile, walked out.

"Where's Joe going?" asked Charlie. "I thought we were going in the boat."

"I think Joe has some things he needs to sort out sweetheart. We'll have to think of something else we can do," said Kate, trying to sound as normal as possible even though her mind was going crazy trying to process what had gone on in just the last few minutes.

"What about Issy? When's she coming back?"

Kate didn't know what to say: she didn't fully understand what was going on herself. Everything had happened so quickly; how was she supposed to explain it to a very confused five-year-old? She had no idea what Joe was thinking, and how long he'd be gone for. Would he be back in a couple of minutes with everything resolved?

She heard tyres on the gravel outside and a moment later there was a knock. Hoping against hope the caller was Arabella bringing Issy back and apologising profusely for taking her in the first place, Kate hurriedly opened the door only to be greeted by the flash of a large camera held by a rather weaselly-looking young man. An older woman of maybe forty stood next to him with a Dictaphone. "Hi Kate," she said cheerfully, "I was wondering if you had a few moments to talk about your relationship with Joseph Wild? Is he here?" she asked, peering around Kate and into the house.

"No, I'm sorry," Kate stammered. "He's not here."

She went to close the door, but the reporter swiftly stuck her foot out into the opening.

"I don't suppose you happen to know where he is?" she asked in a much less friendly tone.

"Nope," replied Kate firmly. "I'm afraid I don't."

The reporter glared at Kate, but sensing she was going to get nowhere, slowly moved her foot. Kate was just shutting the door when Charlie came up from behind her. "You do know where Joe is Mum! He's gone to the barn he's staying in over there," he pointed down the path leading to the two barns. "He said he needed to make a phone call, remember?"

"Thank you very much," said the reporter silkily, before turning on her heel and barking to her photographer, "Follow me," as she marched off in the direction Charlie had pointed.

Kate pushed the door closed with a sigh, hearing more vehicles coming up the drive as she did so. She tried to call Joe to give him a heads up, but his phone was engaged.

There was no point in trying to go out anywhere now. She kept Charlie close by as he still seemed upset and confused by what had gone on, and more so when reporters began ringing the doorbell and calling through the letter box. He kept asking questions Kate simply did not have the answers to: when would Issy be back? Where had she gone? Was Joe coming for lunch?

Cursing the fact her telephone numbers were readily available online for anyone wanting to get in contact about booking to stay, she unplugged the house phone, which had begun ringing constantly with "unknown callers", and kept her mobile in her hand, with the sound off, hoping Joe would at least text to let her know what was going on. She was worried about Issy and anxious to hear the little girl was alright. Of course she was just going to her mother, but to be taken away like that . . .

Half an hour passed, and still Joe hadn't called, messaged or turned up on her doorstep. It seemed everyone else in the world was trying to get through to her though. She turned her mobile off, needing some peace from the flashing screen and the constant vibrations. Joe knew where she was, although she realised him popping round wouldn't be easy given how many reporters and photographers were now crowded outside. She'd closed all the blinds on the windows at the front of the house and was staying in the back.

Kate was feeling pretty fed up: she was a prisoner in her own home because of Joe. Yes, she supposed she'd always known this happening might be a possibility, but that knowledge didn't help with the situation she was now in.

She appreciated Joe was desperately trying to deal with what was going on with Issy, but he could at least check she and Charlie were alright. That wouldn't exactly take him long.

Another half an hour passed. Kate knew she'd feel a lot better if she had Joe with her, or at least knew he was okay and didn't blame her for what had happened. Charlie was also getting a grumpy, he had no idea what was going on, or why everyone was acting so strangely.

Kate had been certain Joe would have returned by now. She didn't feel comfortable with her son being in the house with their front door being knocked on constantly and reporters shouting to them through it. What was wrong with these people? For the second time that day she thought about calling the police. She hadn't wanted to, thinking it might make things worse for Joe, so she waited, wishing she could speak to him, to be reassured herself and to know what he usually did to deal with this. But she had no idea what he was doing. Presumably the police would be able to move everyone away. It was too late to worry about more publicity and making a scene now she considered. She'd have to do something soon; they couldn't carry on like this all day. Charlie still kept asking why there were so many people outside and why they wanted to talk to them. She tried to explain they wanted to speak to her about Joe because he was famous, but the little boy just didn't understand why the reporters wouldn't go away when they didn't answer the door.

Finally, Kate heard at least two more cars pull up outside, followed by raised, authoritative voices barking indistinct commands over the constant background noise of the reporters. A moment or two later and vehicles started up again but then drove away. Kate listened carefully. All seemed quiet. She went into the sitting room and dared a peek around the side of the blinds. Two black Range Rovers were parked in the driveway. A huge man, who could well have been one of Joe's bodyguards she'd seen before in London — she couldn't be quite sure — stood stiffly by the side of one, looking around him grumpily. She assumed there were others in the 4x4s, but she couldn't see through the blacked-out windows.

Cautiously, she went to the front door and opened it. The bodyguard turned to face her. "Ms Holloway," he said calmly.

"Hi," Kate squeaked. "Thank you for getting rid of that lot."

The man nodded in response.

"Are you waiting for Joe?" she asked.

"I'm not at liberty to say," the man said stiffly. Despite everything, Kate fought back a little smile. She'd never have believed she of all people could have ended up in a situation like this.

"Is it safe for me to come out of my house?" she asked.

"Certainly ma'am," came the reply.

Kate did a quick check for herself and then called Charlie out. He was still a little nervous as he peeped round the door so Kate encouraged him gently, "Don't worry sweetie, they've all gone now."

"Will they come back again?"

"I don't know," Kate answered truthfully. "But hopefully not."

The bodyguard spoke into his walkie-talkie. "Sorry ma'am," he then said to Kate. "I'm going to have to ask you to return inside."

Kate hurried Charlie back indoors and closed the front door again. It appeared the assault on their home wasn't quite as over as she had thought.

There was another knock almost immediately. "Apparently your mother is here and would like to see you. She's been stopped at the turning from the road."

"Well, let her through!" said Kate in exasperation.

"Could you give me a description of your mother and her car please ma'am?"

Only once Kate had given a full description did the man give permission for a very fretful Susie to drive up the lane to the house.

"Are you alright?" Kate's mother asked her immediately, enveloping her daughter in a hug. "It's absolutely dreadful. Haven't they got anything better to do than badger the man?"

Seeing Charlie standing next to his mum, she quickly put a smile on her face. "Hello Charlie! I didn't spot you; I bet you're having a funny old day aren't you?"

"I am Granny," replied Charlie, solemnly.

"I thought I'd come and check you and Mummy are alright."

"We're fine, Mum," said Kate. "Though it's been pretty crazy."

"I tried calling for ages but couldn't get through on the house line."

"Sorry Mum, I should have texted you or something. The phone was just going crazy with reporters who'd got the number from the website or somewhere so I unplugged it. Then the same thing happened with my mobile so I switched it off. I didn't mean to worry you. I think Charlie here could do with a bit of cheering up. Issy's gone to stay with her mum. It was all rather sudden," she explained, giving her mum a look to let her know she'd explain properly later when the little boy wasn't around.

"Right, why don't I take Charlie over to my house," Kate's mum suggested. "Give you and Joe a chance to work out what to do to make sure those nasty reporters don't come back again. Is he here?" she asked, craning round Kate, just realising Joe was nowhere to be seen.

"He's in his barn," Kate explained. "If you could watch Charlie for a bit here so I could go and talk to him . . ."

"I'm afraid that won't be possible ma'am," came the deep voice of the bodyguard. "You and your son need to remain on the property."

"What?!" said Kate. After the day she'd had, she'd just about had enough of being told what to do, and she was damned if she was going to let someone else dictate her actions.

Kate's mum waded in before matters escalated, "I'll take Charlie inside and you can go over to the barn and talk to

Joe," she placated. "Would that be alright? She won't really be leaving, will she? It's still in the grounds of her house," she said pointedly to the bodyguard, who spoke into his walkie-talkie, then nodded to the affirmative.

* * *

Kate would usually just walk straight into the barn, but she knocked now. There was a pause before she heard the gruff, "Come in."

Joe was sat, hunched over, on the sofa, his head in his hands. His mobile phone was on the table set on speaker. Everything about him radiated hostility.

"How dare you subject our child to the paparazzi!" Kate heard Genevieve screech down the phone.

"I didn't! It's a complete misunderstanding," said Joe irately.

"Oh really. Well, it looks to me like you got a bit fed up of not being in the limelight, and decided to use our daughter to gain yourself some free publicity."

"Don't be ridiculous Genevieve; you know it's always been me fighting to keep Issy out of the papers."

"Her name is Ismene!"

"Look, I'm sorry she's been dragged into the news. It won't happen again."

"You're right, it won't. I'm not going to let it. Ismene will be staying with me. My lawyers will be in touch about more permanent arrangements."

"Genevieve, be reasonable . . ." begged Joe, his voice rising with his frustration, but she'd hung up. Evidently, for her at least, their conversation was at an end.

Joe shook his head and looked down at the phone in disbelief, before putting it in his pocket. He took a deep breath and turned to Kate, not giving her a chance to speak before growling, "Did you call the papers?"

"No! Of course not!" Kate retorted instantly, hurt.

"Well, someone must have."

"Well, it wasn't me!"

"What about your mum, or Becca?"

"You know they wouldn't!"

"Do I?" he snapped.

"Yes," said Kate firmly. "And to be honest, I can't believe you're accusing them!"

Joe momentarily looked shamefaced, but swiftly recovered himself enough to blurt out, "They could have let something slip accidently, or maybe it was Nick? Would he do it?"

"No!"

"From what you've said he's none too keen on me being around."

"Of course he doesn't like you being here! He's my ex-husband! But he wouldn't do it."

"How can you be so sure?"

"Because I know him, I was married to him for goodness' sake!"

"Who else could have done it?"

"I don't know!" She took a second to mentally step back and focus on constructively handling things, rather than letting the argument develop. "Why don't we go out for a while? Get some fresh air and work out what to do?"

"Go where? How are we supposed to get out? They'll all be waiting for us at the road." He walked across the room, running his fingers through his hair in frustration. "I'll get my stuff together, I'm going to have to leave."

"Right now?"

"I said I would if the press got wind of where I was. I can't bring you and Charlie into all this craziness. And I need to get Issy back."

"If you let Genevieve calm down a bit, maybe she'll be more willing to talk. You can do that from here," Kate said, trying to be reasonable.

"Genevieve won't be happy about that."

"You can't just do whatever she tells you to."

"I will if that's what it takes for her to let me see Issy."
He got out his mobile; his call was answered almost instantly.
"Hi, how quickly can you get here? Okay. Bye."

He turned to Kate. "I'd better pack, my car will be here
to pick me up soon."

"Where will you go?"

"I don't know yet, I'll make some calls."

"Couldn't you at least wait until you've got a bit more of
a plan? There's no need to rush off. We need to talk."

"It's better I go now. The longer I leave it, the more paps
will turn up."

"But Charlie will be devastated if you leave without saying goodbye."

Joe went quiet. "I'm sorry, but I think it's for the best."

"So I guess this is it then," said Kate softly, numb and
disbelieving at how the last few minutes had unfolded; the
handful of moments it had taken for the heartbreaking col-
lapse of their fledgling relationship.

"I guess so," he said coldly, and left the room.

Kate sat down to steady herself. How could everything
have changed so suddenly? And why was Joe so angry with
her? It was ridiculous; she'd done nothing wrong, but felt he
was punishing her for what had happened. The unhelpful
voice of her conscience whispered that she shouldn't have let
Issy go; she should have found some way to stop her being
taken. Tears filled her eyes. But she fought the urge to blame
herself: there wasn't anything she could have done. And she
hadn't done anything wrong here either.

The way Joe was treating her was just so unjust. She'd
told him she'd had absolutely nothing to do with the news
story, why didn't he believe her? She'd trust him if the situation were reversed, she was sure she would. How could his
feelings towards her have shifted so drastically? Had he ever
even cared about her? No, that was unfair she admonished
herself: they'd had something together she was certain. Joe
hadn't led her on, but they couldn't have been in the same

"place" she thought, else he wouldn't have given it all up as easily as he had. He would have at least tried to hold onto her.

But then, Kate reminded herself, she hadn't been dealing with the paparazzi for years and it wasn't her child who was being kept from her. What was Genevieve thinking? She must know Joe would never do anything to put Issy in harm's way, he adored his little girl. Was this just some kind of horrible power play? A ploy to get control over Joe again? Kate really couldn't think of any other explanation.

* * *

Kate felt no less miserable almost a week later, though, thankfully, she hadn't seen any paparazzi for a while, and had gladly accepted her mum's offer to take Charlie out for a couple of hours. Worried that journalists might still be hanging around nearby, they'd just been skulking indoors and Charlie was going a little stir crazy without Issy to keep him entertained. But no sooner had Susie driven off with Charlie, than Nick turned up.

Kate went to the front door to meet him. "Hey," she said, as cheerfully as she could manage. "How was your work trip? Are you here for Charlie? Did I forget something? I thought you weren't having him until Saturday?"

"No, don't panic. I just thought I'd pop by and check how you both are. The trip was fine; I got back late last night."

"Come on through," said Kate, leading the way into the kitchen and putting the kettle on. "You saw the papers then . . ."

"Yeah, of course," Nick admitted, "I've been meaning to call, but I thought it would be awkward with Joe here . . ."

"He left."

"I know. They're saying he's in France now."

With Genevieve, Kate added silently to herself.

"Are you alright?" Nick asked awkwardly.

"I guess so," Kate answered with a shrug. "It's a lesson learnt I suppose."

"So it's all over between you two?"

"Yep."

"I'm sorry," Nick said. Seeing the surprise on Kate's face he continued, "I know I wasn't exactly thrilled about you seeing him to begin with. It was really strange hearing Charlie chatting about another guy, a father figure, but the first time that happened was always going to be rough."

Kate nodded, "It's definitely going to be weird when you introduce him to a woman you're seeing."

"If I ever meet anyone else…"

"Of course you will! And she'll be wonderful."

Nick smiled, "Thank you, but my point is that it was my problem, Joe didn't do anything wrong, and it sounds like you two were good together."

"I thought we were," Kate said, blinking furiously as she felt tears beginning to build up.

"Come here," said Nick pulling her into a hug. "The guy's an idiot to have let you go, and if he can't see that he doesn't deserve you."

"Thanks, Nick."

"Anytime."

* * *

Kate continued going about her day as best as she could, trying as usual to avoid thinking about Joe as much as possible. The weather was miserable, which made outdoor jobs a no-no, and she was determined to stay away from Joe's barn at all costs, even though she ought to give it a good clean now he'd gone so it would be ready for its next occupant.

She sat down at her desk to pay some bills and her gaze fell on the photo of Charlie in front of her. She looked at her son, at his goofy grin and floppy hair. She was so grateful for the friendship she had with Nick and their co-parenting of Charlie together. These thoughts automatically led her back to Joe's situation. Despite his actions, she could only imagine how he felt, wondering how much access he was going to have to his own daughter; how much of a part he was going to be able to play in her life. The fact that his own father had walked away from him when he was growing up . . . well . . . that was without doubt affecting how he saw things now.

Kate exhaled, letting go off some of the hurt and anger she'd been bottling up along with the air.

How could Genevieve behave the way she was about those photographs? However angry she was, and however badly their marriage had ended, she must know Joe was a good dad, and that it was hugely important for Ismene to spend time with her father.

What Genevieve needed was someone who'd be honest with her about her behaviour, and what potentially terrible repercussions there could be from it for Issy.

There was a knock on the front door, and Kate got up with a frown, she wasn't expecting anyone: no one was booked into either of the barns until the weekend, and she hadn't reopened the campsite, not having had the energy to deal with the logistics.

She opened the door a tiny amount and tentatively peered round it, worried the press were back to hound her again. She was surprised to find the woman who'd left Cherry Barn early, Julia, on her doorstep.

"Oh, hi," Kate said. "Did you forget something?"

"Julia Brazer, *Daily News*. Kate, I'm here to make you a very generous offer for the story of what went on between you and Joseph Wild. Tell me, do you have any regrets about stealing a married man away from his loving family?"

"It was you . . . You're a reporter. You took the pictures of Issy," said Kate slowly, as the whole mystery of the tabloid photos began to unfold within her mind, "But how did you know they were here?"

"Let's just say a rather bitter little bird told me. How do you feel about the news that Genevieve Moore plans to obtain a court order banning Joseph Wild from access to their daughter except for supervised, fortnightly visits?" Julia continued.

Genevieve, Kate knew. Genevieve had set Joe up, as revenge for him starting a relationship with her.

Kate calmly closed the door in Julia's face. She had absolutely nothing to say to her — though a horrible person, Julia was merely a tool. Kate turned the lock, and put the chain across before going into the kitchen and opening up her laptop. There must be a way to get through to Genevieve and convince her to change her mind. She had to appeal to what was important to Genevieve, and, from what Joe had said, that wasn't her daughter, it was her career.

In order to speak to Genevieve, Kate first had to find out her phone number, which was unlikely to be easy. Arabella clearly wasn't going to be any help, but didn't take long for Kate to find the name of Genevieve's agent, along with her contact details. Before she could think better of it, Kate called the number on the website. It rang twice before it was answered, "Miranda Hart's office, Sarah speaking".

"Hello," said Kate. She definitely should have thought this conversation through more. "I need to contact Genevieve Moore, and was wondering if you could put me in contact with her."

"Any business matters for Ms Moore need to come through our office," Sarah said. "Can I take some details?"

"It's not really a business matter. . ." Kate admitted.

"I'm afraid Ms Moore is a very busy woman," replied Sarah, her voice firmer. "But if you'd like to provide me with your address, I'm sure she'd be happy to send you a signed photo."

"No, thank you," said Kate. "And thank you for your time."

"Thank you for your call," replied Sarah, and the line went dead.

Kate sighed and walked straight upstairs to her bedroom. Taking down a suitcase from the top of her wardrobe, she began to pack. It was time to execute Plan B: she was going to find Genevieve and appeal to her in person.

* * *

When Susie arrived a while later with Charlie in tow, Kate was almost ready to leave.

"Mum," said Kate, turning to Susie. "Can you look after Charlie again for me?"

"Of course, sweetheart, anytime. It'll do you good to get out. When would you like me to have him?"

"Um, now?"

"Now?" she repeated.

"Yep," said Kate, decisiveness coursing through her. "There's someone I need to talk to, and I think it needs to be in person."

"Is it Joe?" asked Susie hopefully. "Has he been in touch? Is he coming back?"

"No, Mum, but it is to do with him. I'm actually going to see Genevieve."

"Genevieve?! But isn't she in France?"

"Yes, I'll be back as soon as I can."

"But why would you want to talk to that awful woman, after all she's done?"

"Because she has Issy. Regardless of what happened between me and Joe, it's not right that he isn't getting to see his daughter. He's a good father, and he deserves proper access to her. I know who took those photographs, and I'm certain the trail leads back to Genevieve."

"That's very decent of you darling, but I'm sure Joe wouldn't expect it, especially after the way he left things."

"I know," said Kate sadly. "But it's not just about him. Genevieve turned my life upside down, made Charlie and I prisoners in our own home. There's nothing I can do to change any of that, but I have to stand up for myself. I've got to do what's right — for Issy as much as for Joe. She needs to have her dad in her life. Someone has to confront Genevieve."

"I'm proud of you," said Susie, coming over and wrapping her daughter in a tight embrace. "Go, and don't worry about Charlie at all. He'll be fine with me."

"Thank you so much, Mum."

Kate quickly finished packing everything she thought she'd need in her somewhat frazzled state. She had to completely focus, otherwise she'd be giving her brain too much time to think about Joe, about how much he'd hurt her. Passport, phone, purse; passport, phone purse, she repeated to herself — anything else she could pick up on her journey.

Her mum and Charlie gave her a lift to the train station. Giving her son a kiss, and a huge cuddle goodbye, she explained she'd see him in a couple of days and was soon on her way.

* * *

Several long hours of travelling and restless mental turmoil later, having booked a flight to Nice on route, she arrived at Gatwick airport. She had a while to wait before her flight left — time to work out where she needed to go to find Genevieve once she was in France.

Kate settled herself down in the corner of a coffee chain outlet with a large cup of tea and got out her mobile. She was going to check every one of the magazines and papers she knew Joe loathed, the ones paying the photographers who followed Genevieve around everywhere she went, in the hope that something she saw might tell her exactly where her nemesis was. She typed "Genevieve Moore France" into each of the publications' search bars and scanned every recent article or photo that came up for clues. She wrote down the names of any towns, restaurants or shops Genevieve had been spotted at, and the date when she was seen there, googling each place in turn. However, it soon became apparent the actress was moving around a fairly large area, presumably filming location shots. And Kate didn't have an infinite amount of time in which to track her down; she had to get back to Charlie as soon as she could.

Kate racked her brains, trying to think of some other way she could find out where Genevieve was. She didn't know any of the woman's friends, and even if she did, they wouldn't give Kate any information, especially once she told them who she was.

Local people might be able to tell her where the star was based, she mused hopefully. It would be a pretty big deal to have a huge Hollywood blockbuster being filmed near you and not something that would go unnoticed.

But, and this was the biggest but, if she did somehow find exactly where Genevieve was, and she did somehow manage to get there, on set, how on earth was she actually going to get to speak to the world-famous, Golden- Globe-nominated actress Genevieve Moore? She was hardly just going to be standing around, waiting for her ex-husband's ex-girlfriend to come and have a little chat with her!

This was the problem with having time to think thought Kate wryly, it gives you the opportunity to slow down and realise what you're attempting is completely stupid.

The emotions of indecision, despair and foolishness all battled it out for supremacy as she sat there. Tired, alone and despondent, she fought back her tears. What was she doing here? What did she think she was going to achieve, really?

The tannoy announced her flight, disrupting the mounting momentum of self-pity and doubt. Much longer and she may very well have decided to turn right around and head back home, but she had her ticket and passport, and here she was — and as silly as she might be being, she'd feel even worse, and more the fool, if she ran away now.

Dragging her suitcase behind her she approached the gate on autopilot. As she found her seat on the plane, she told herself with assumed firmness — trying to recreate her earlier determination and purpose — that as she'd come this far she really may as well see things through. She was on the plane, and on her way, and that was that. She'd been travelling for hours now, so she'd use the short flight for a little sleep and then come up with a plan for tracking down exactly where Genevieve was once she was in Nice.

She could do this. She could.

CHAPTER THIRTEEN

Kate woke up as the aeroplane was preparing to land, feeling slightly more refreshed, and definitely more able to face the problems ahead.

She opened the shutter on her window, hoping to catch a glimpse of the coast, but found it was far too dark to make out practically anything. It was also much too late to begin seeking out Genevieve, even if she'd had an idea of where to start. She'd find a hotel, get a bite to eat and go to bed. Then she would get up early and scour the region.

Stepping out of the airport and into the chilled night air, she steeled herself to draw on her schoolgirl French — not used in well over a decade — in order to sort out somewhere to stay and marched towards the taxi rank.

"*Bonjour!*" she said brightly to a friendly looking cab driver, then wondered whether after ten o'clock at night could really still be counted as "*jour*".

"*Bonsoir*, madame," replied the man pleasantly.

"*Soir*! That's the word I was looking for, thought Kate with a smile. "*Voulez-vous . . .*" Kate began hesitantly.

"Would you rather we speak English, madame?" interrupted the man gently. He was short and rather rotund, with dark hair and eyes. Kate guessed he must be in his late fifties.

He appeared just about as much an archetypal Frenchman as was possible and didn't fit at all with the image of the glamorous Côte d'Azur she had in her mind. He looked more like he belonged running a small vineyard in the middle of nowhere alongside his rosy cheeked, scolding wife.

Laughing with relief, Kate replied, "Oh yes please! I think it would be easier for both of us!"

"I think so too. Where can I take you?"

"A hotel please. Do you know somewhere nice, but not too expensive?"

"Of course, madame."

"Thank you so much," Kate climbed in the taxi and sank back gratefully into the comfortable passenger seat while the driver put her bag into the boot.

"My name is Thierry," he offered.

"I'm Kate."

"What brings you to Nice?" he asked, turning down the radio, muting a rather intense sounding debate taking place in very rapid French.

"It's a long story, but basically I'm looking for someone," explained Kate after a pause.

"Oh?"

"Someone rather famous actually: Genevieve Moore."

Thierry didn't say anything, so Kate added, "She's an actress, from Hollywood."

"I know who Genevieve Moore is," said Thierry. "Why do you want to see her? Are you a big fan?"

"Um, no not really," said Kate honestly. "I'm trying to get in touch with her for a friend."

"This must be a very important friend."

"He is," said Kate quietly.

"Ah, a man," said the driver wisely, tutting and shaking his head in commiseration.

"I'm afraid so."

"Would you like to tell me about it? I am a good listener."

Kate unexpectedly found that she did need to talk, needed to get what had happened off her chest, to someone completely uninvolved. Once she started, it all tumbled out; from the distant past and Joe's arrival at her sixth form, to his furious departure from her life. She told Thierry about Julia and the reporters, and Genevieve's orchestration of the newspaper photographs.

Eventually her cathartic outpouring finished and there was silence in the cab. Thierry cleared his throat, then paused, clearly deliberating with himself, "I know where you can find Genevieve Moore."

"You do? Where?" asked Kate incredulously. Was this some ploy to try to get more money out of her?

"My brother. He is also a taxi driver. He's been working for the film company Moore is with. He hasn't met her, she has her own private car and driver, but he will know where they are filming each day."

Kate's heart felt like it had jumped into her mouth. Serendipity? Or con? Surely, she thought, if Thierry was planning on stringing her along then that would soon be very obvious she thought. And ascribing him a darker motive seemed ridiculous outside film and fiction, not to say unfair and terribly uncharitable given his compassion. As unlikely as this break seemed, could she afford not to pursue it?

In actuality she hesitated only a second before deciding she had to trust this man. It looked like fate might well have thrown her a line, and she was going to grab it. But she'd make sure she wrote down the taxi number and texted it to Becca just in case.

"Can you take me to the film set tomorrow?" she asked.

"*Certainement.* I'll pick you up at nine in the morning. I will find out where they are from my brother tonight, but he said they were planning on staying in the same spot for a few weeks now. They have finished the outdoor shoots and have moved into a studio. It's about thirty minutes' drive from the hotel I am taking you to."

"Thank you very much. I so appreciate this."

"I think you are a good person. I am happy to help you."

Thierry pulled up outside a large, whitewashed building. The lamps on its facade illuminated the huge tubs of flowers adorning its courtyard and the gloriously overflowing hanging baskets, surreal in the artificial light, surrounding the wooden door.

"This is your hotel. It is owned by my aunt and uncle. They will treat you well."

"Thank you," said Kate, handing over the fare due — which she was sure was less that it should be. "You've been so kind."

"It is not a problem," replied Thierry, with a fatherly smile. He retrieved her bag. "Come this way."

He led her to the entrance and knocked. Waiting a moment, he was just about to try knocking again when the door was opened by a tiny woman with long, silver hair. Her face instantly broke into a smile, and she and Thierry kissed each other on both cheeks. Their brief conversation was well beyond Kate's understanding. Thierry's "All is well. I will see you tomorrow morning," as he left, did nothing to help clarify where things stood.

"*Bonsoir*," said Kate nervously, before deciding to take a chance with English rather than having to resort to sign language when her very poor French made absolutely no sense to the poor woman at all. "I need a room for the night?"

"Of course, of course!" the old lady replied in a thick accent, ushering Kate inside.

Kate was taken into a roomy reception area with a terracotta tiled floor and a desk, behind which sat an elderly man who resembled Thierry greatly, but looked maybe twenty years older.

"I am Nicole," the woman explained pleasantly. "And this is my husband, Marc."

She spoke in rapid French to her husband, Kate made out Thierry's name but little else.

"Let me show you to your room," Nicole said to Kate. "And then would you like something to eat?"

"That would be wonderful, thank you," said Kate, gratefully. Despite her doze on the plane, she was exhausted and it was good to know she had somewhere to sleep, the offer of food, and most importantly, that she'd be seeing Genevieve in the morning.

Kate was led up two flights of stairs by Nicole, who, regardless of Kate's protestations and dismay, insisted upon carrying her bag for her, and into a single room with a sloping ceiling. It smelt of wood and furniture polish, and the window opposite the bed looked out over the building's large, flood-lit patioed garden. If it wasn't for the faint noise of traffic and the snatches of conversation drifting up from the streets below, Kate would have found it hard to imagine she was in a city at all. The room had a small en suite attached, the door of which was so low even Kate had to stoop a little to walk through it. It contained a toilet, a sink and a shower: it was perfect for the night. She tidied herself up a bit and then went back downstairs.

Nicole fussed over Kate, checking that everything was fine with her room, and ushered her into the hotel's bar area, where despite the late hour, some of the other patrons were still gathered. They smiled in welcome. Kate was shown to a table and Marc appeared with a glass of red wine, quickly followed with a plate of delicious bread served with two cheeses, herb covered olives and thick cut ham. The food was amazing, Kate just wished that her first visit to France since childhood was in somewhat more relaxed circumstances, and she had someone to enjoy it with.

By the time she'd finished eating it was close to midnight, but the other customers in the bar were displaying no signs of heading up to bed. Some watched a small television in a corner, others chatted to Marc who'd remained behind the bar and looked most at home there.

Nicole came to and fro, chatting to Kate as she worked about how long she and Marc had run the hotel and tales of their experiences doing so. The wine was delicious but served to make Kate feel even sleepier than she already had been. Finally she had to admit defeat; she could keep her eyes open no longer, and excused herself.

The single bed in her room was unbelievably soft and comfortable. She lay down, exhausted.

The emotional and physical toll of the day left little room for introspection. So tonight, for the first night in days, she fell asleep in moments, barely dwelling on the hollow inside her and how much she missed Joe and wished with all her heart that he was with her.

* * *

True to his word, Thierry was ready to go at nine the next morning. Kate had brought her bag down to the reception at eight thirty, hoping to grab a coffee before she went outside to meet him, only to find the man himself sat enjoying breakfast in the bar. He insisted she join him, and Nicole came over bringing Kate strong, hot coffee and flaky, warm croissants with butter and jam. Nicole looked as fresh as a daisy despite how late she must have been up working the previous night.

At nine, Thierry took the last sip of his drink and declared, "I think it is time for us to get going."

They walked out to the car together and Thierry put Kate's bag in the boot again. The day was chilly and cloudy, but, as Kate took a last look at the hotel, it nevertheless appeared bright and cheerful. She promised herself she'd come back here someday; maybe treat her mum and Charlie.

"I spoke to my brother," Thierry explained, "And they are still filming at the studios, just outside the city. He can get you past security and onto the lot where they are shooting, but the rest . . ." he shrugged his shoulders apologetically. "Do you have a plan?"

"I'll wing it," she said with false confidence. "Thank you so much, Thierry. I honestly don't know what I would have done if I hadn't bumped into you outside the airport yesterday."

"You would have thought of something," Thierry said with a smile. "You are a resourceful woman. I wish you luck."

* * *

Thierry pulled up five hundred metres from the studios, next to another taxi with an almost identical driver. Dark, round and jovial, Victor could have been Thierry's twin — perhaps just a little more lined and a smidge tubbier about the middle.

With a cheerful "*Bonjour!*" to Kate, Victor launched into a rapid, incomprehensible exchange in French with his brother before signalling to her to get in the back of his cab; Thierry climbed in the front.

At the gate, the guards and Victor greeted each other with much bonhomie; he perfunctorily flourished his pass, and they were idly waved through. Kate let out a deep breath she hadn't realised she'd been holding.

Getting her attention, Victor pointed to a cluster of buildings in the distance with a big '2' painted on the side of the largest.

"My brother says Genevieve is filming over there," Thierry confirmed. "We will wait here for you." He reached onto the back seat for his newspaper.

"Are you sure?"

"It is no problem. My brother will chat to me. I haven't seen him for a while. Take your time," the Frenchman replied calmly, winding down his window and pulling out a pack of *Gauloises* from the glove compartment. "I know you will do well. *Bonne chance*, Kate."

Getting out of the car, Kate wished some of Thierry's composure would seep into her. She walked as confidently as she could towards the large hangers but had no idea what she was going to do once she got to them. She hoped she wouldn't need to try to talk her way inside with her grasp of the language. Maybe she ought to go back to the car and ask Thierry to come with her so he could at least be her interpreter. But he'd already rescued her enough, she couldn't really expect him to do more for her, and she didn't want him or his brother to get into trouble for aiding her. No, she'd have to deal with this by herself.

As she got closer to the lot Victor had told her to head for, there were several trailers and Portakabins dotted around the larger buildings which she saw had notices and direction arrows on, presumably saying what was being done where. They were naturally in French, but she hoped she'd be able to make out enough to point her in the direction of the correct "stage", if that was even the word for what she was looking for.

Each step was a little more nerve-wracking than the last. In the taxi, approaching the studios, she'd been completely divided: half of her thought she was being crazy, there was no point in being here and no way she was ever going to get anywhere near this mega movie star; the other half of her knew she had to try, she'd never forgive herself if she didn't. Only, right here, right now, all by herself, it was getting harder and harder to remember that later half, and her excellent reasons for doing this.

But the remains of her determination whispered: someone had to stand up to Genevieve and tell her the way she behaved was not acceptable; she couldn't just trample over people to get what she wanted! And it genuinely wasn't all about Kate, or Joe — as much as she knew she still loved him, and in all probability always would — she was thinking about Issy, who she'd really come to care about in the short time she'd known her. She couldn't stand by and watch that little girl's relationship with her father be destroyed. Not if there was the faintest possibility there was something she could do to help.

Then, she stopped. How was this going to work, exactly? First, she told Genevieve what a horrid person she was, and then she instructed her to do the decent thing with her daughter? A woman like Genevieve would never acknowledge her mistakes, and as for listening to criticism . . . what was she thinking?

Damn it! There was a choice to be made wasn't there? She could try and have her confrontation, or she could try to help Issy and Joe.

Kate knew what was important.

* * *

168

In trying to plan her next move, Kate didn't notice the group of people approaching her from behind until she heard a gruff American accent, "Excuse me, lady, have you got a pass?" and she realised the request was being directed at her. She turned round and was faced with a group of rather serious looking men in suits, all holding walkie-talkies and glaring at her.

"Oh, I'm terribly sorry, I appear to have mislaid it," she said rather primly, suddenly becoming extremely British. What was she going to do now? They were sure to escort her out immediately as soon as they realised she wasn't supposed to be there.

But before any of the men could question her further, a rather shrill female voice called out from behind the convoy, "What exactly is the hold up? I'm supposed to be getting back to my trailer and resting in between takes! I'm simply drained from the intensity of my performance."

"Genevieve!" squeaked Kate, involuntarily.

The diva herself pushed her way past the men to stand in front of Kate. "Yes?" she enquired, squinting at Kate, clearly trying to recall where she knew her from. Then it clicked, and her squint turned to a scowl, "What do you want?" she growled.

"I need to talk to you," said Kate, sounding far calmer than she actually felt. "It won't take long."

Genevieve hesitated.

"Do you need us to remove this person, Ms Moore?" asked the largest of the security men.

Before Genevieve could reply, Kate said softly, "I don't think you want to do this here, in public. Joe and I talked a lot, Genevieve, and I never signed any confidentiality agreement."

China-blue eyes regarded her frostily, considering, "Fine. You've got five minutes."

Genevieve marched into a trailer, evidently expecting Kate to follow in her wake. Kate paused, then walked up the steps and through the door the movie star had left swung open.

Genevieve draped herself on a chaise longue, sipping from a bottle of San Peregrino held in one hand, and massaging her temple with the other.

"Okay, what do you want?" she demanded. "This really isn't a convenient time."

"Then I'll get straight to the point," Kate said, committing to the decision she'd reached outside, "I'm here to talk about Ismene."

"What exactly has my daughter got to do with you?"

"She's a lovely little girl, and I care about her."

Genevieve sneered. "You mean you want her father back?"

"This isn't about me," said Kate, struggling not to tell Genevieve exactly what she thought of her.

Genevieve didn't respond, so Kate quickly continued, "Joe's a good man Genevieve, and a good father. This is hurting him."

"A good father wouldn't have subjected his daughter to the paparazzi," replied Genevieve coldly.

"I've spoken to Julia. We both know Joe had nothing to do with those photos."

Genevieve appeared momentarily ruffled, but swiftly composed herself, "And?"

"I'm not here to out you. I've got no interest in doing that unless I'm forced to. I want to help Issy. It's wrong for Ismene and Joe to be kept apart."

Sensing she wasn't getting anywhere, Kate decided to try a different approach. "I know you grew up without a father, Genevieve. However things are between you and Joe, you don't want that for Ismene."

Genevieve still looked angry, but there might have been a waver in her steely self-possession.

"Ismene loves him so much," Kate continued tentatively, "and it can't be easy for you looking after her by yourself. I'm a single mum too. I know how hard it can be. Joe could really help you. It's tough trying to have a career and look after a child."

"Especially with the sort of work I do," mused Genevieve. "It's so taxing, I give *so* much to my art."

"I can only imagine . . ." muttered Kate, determined to keep her on this track and not say anything that could upset her. However much she wanted to tell Genevieve exactly what she thought of her and her actions, that wouldn't help anyone.

"Maybe you're right," conceded the actress. "I need to be thinking about myself more, putting me first."

"Absolutely, but it's so hard, isn't it?"

Genevieve looked at Kate closely. Again, she screwed up her eyes slightly, as if trying to work out whether Kate was serious. Kate kept her face a perfect mask.

Satisfied, Genevieve replied, "Exactly." The actress drummed her impeccably manicured fingers on the arm of the seat. "Ismene has been very . . . demanding this last week. And now that my boyfriend Sergey is back, of course it's hard to find the time to . . ." The drumming continued, then stopped. "Motherhood is a terrible burden. And it's most unfair that Joseph expects me to shoulder as much of it as he does. Men forget that they have parenting responsibilities too and women need to make them face up to these responsibilities."

The blue eyes again locked with Kate's — whether challenging Kate to call her on the brazen lies or merely gauging her audience's response, Kate couldn't tell. Evidently deciding that she liked the sound of this version of the "truth", Genevieve continued. "I'll have my assistant speak to Joseph. Ismene can be with him until I finish shooting." Getting up she concluded, "Now, I need to concentrate on my character. I really must get back on set, our director can't do without me."

Kate watched Genevieve swish out of the trailer. The woman was unbelievable! Though she certainly has chutzpah, Kate thought; she had to give her that!

She felt her body relax as the tension of the situation evaporated. She'd done it! She, Kate Holloway, had actually succeeded in this ludicrous, harebrained scheme! Despite the odds, she'd somehow found Genevieve and — overcoming her own pride — managed to talk the self-centred prima donna into doing the right thing for someone other than just herself. Kate's righteous indignation had got her here, but she'd been able to look past the anger, to be the "bigger" person, and so help Issy. And help Joe. She'd done the best she could for him. And always would.

CHAPTER FOURTEEN

An exhausted Kate very gratefully turned the key in her front door late that night. When she'd spoken to her mum to see how she and Charlie were, Susie had suggested staying another night in France, but Kate wanted to get back. Her mum would drop Charlie home tomorrow, and they'd have the whole day together with no guests booked in until the following afternoon.

Dumping her bags in the hallway, Kate went into the kitchen. The answer phone was flashing with messages, the majority she knew would still be from reporters. She'd check them at some point. Now she just wanted a shower followed by a cup of tea and her bed.

* * *

She almost didn't hear the quiet tap on the front door over the noise of the kettle boiling. What was this? Not the damn paparazzi again she hoped, glad she'd thought to lock the door behind her.

"Who is it?" she called out. She didn't want to be photographed standing exhausted on the threshold.

"It's Joe," a voice replied. "Can I come in?"

Kate couldn't help rushing to open the door, and felt a wave of sympathy for Joe when she saw him: he looked as tired as she felt. But she pulled herself up sharply: he'd hurt her, she must stop feeling sorry for him.

"I need to talk to you," Joe said quietly.

"Charlie's not here," Kate said, realising why Joe was keeping his voice down.

"Oh," Joe replied, and continued speaking at a normal volume. "Kate, I wanted you to know Genevieve's done a complete U-turn, Issy's going to live with me. She'll still see her mum of course, in the holidays and when Genevieve's not working, but I'll have primary custody."

"That's great news, Joe, I'm really glad everything worked out for you."

He looked uncomfortable. "I know you went to speak to her. I'm not sure what you said, but thank you. From Issy and me."

Kate tried to look casual. "What Genevieve was doing was wrong; I couldn't stand by and not do anything. Even with how things ended with us."

He flushed at this. "I'm . . . so sorry about that. I was an ass." He rubbed the back of his neck as he went on sheepishly, "I completely overreacted about the journalists finding out where I was and taking those photographs." He looked at her pleadingly, "And of course I know it wasn't you or your family who told them."

"Yes. Well. I'm glad you can see that now!" said Kate, crossly.

Joe took her hands. "I understand you're angry, but please hear me out?" Kate nodded, and he continued, "I love you, Kate. I knew I was in love with you, even before that day we spent sailing. And this time apart . . . it's shown me what you mean to me — I want you. I want to be with you."

"Why did you leave then?"

"I was terrified I was going to lose Issy, I couldn't think about anything else. I wanted to protect you and Charlie too, and I was furious about what had happened. I had to calm

Genevieve down and make her see reason — she was so livid the photos were taken, and believed you, or someone close to you, was to blame. I thought if I left here it would take the reporters away and show Genevieve how important Issy was to me. If I did what she wanted, made her feel she'd won . . . I wasn't setting out to end it between us, I didn't think of it like that. I don't know . . . I was so worked up, it all got out of control, got away from me."

"But when you'd calmed down, why didn't you get in touch? Let me know you were alright, tell me what was going on?"

Joe paused before replying, shuffling his feet in shame-faced self-consciousness. "I was embarrassed, so embarrassed by how I'd treated you and your family and Becca. Especially after everything you'd done for me. I accused you all of doing a horrible thing . . . I know none of you would ever have sold me out to the papers. I guess being with Genevieve . . . well, some of the melodrama seems to have rubbed off on me. As soon as I'd left, I realised how badly I'd behaved, that I had to apologise and make amends, but I couldn't come to visit in case the press ended up back on your doorstep. And I didn't see how I could make things right over the phone, even if you would have picked up. I didn't know what to say or where to start. I'm an idiot."

"You weren't completely wrong blaming me," Kate sighed. "Julia — the woman who was staying in Cherry Barn — took the photos. I should have realised she was a journalist. Her booking the whole house midweek just for herself and she asked so many questions — it didn't really add up. And, well, I didn't think. If I hadn't agreed to her staying, she never would have got the pictures."

"No, you're wrong. Of course she would have got the pictures, even without staying here. None of them were actually taken on your property were they? She got them when we went out for the day. And she booked the barn knowing that I was staying in the other one. She must have done."

"Yes, she did." It was Kate's turn to feel foolish. "When she called to make the reservation, she checked the other barn would still have the same person staying in it. It didn't click at the time that it was a bit weird she'd ask that."

"So she must have known I was staying here when she called up. She'd been tipped off by someone. But the only reason she got the photos of us was because I got us to all go out together in public. In the circumstances, I knew better than that. I was daft. I took a chance. It was my fault."

"No," said Kate deciding to tell him all. "It wasn't you, Joe. It was Genevieve — she tipped off Julia about where you were. And where Issy was."

Joe's lips pursed as he processed what she'd just revealed. "It makes sense. Classic Genevieve," he said tiredly. "She would have seen the photos as an easy way to make me look bad. Garner sympathy and get her some column inches. And if it came to a custody battle for Issy in court . . ." His shoulders shrugged. "It looks like she was ready to use it there too — irresponsible parenting, claim I was the one using Issy for publicity. How she had to step in to 'protect her daughter'."

"I don't understand how she could do it to Issy."

"She won't have thought about it in those terms. You might have noticed everything has to revolve around her and her needs. She wouldn't actually have set out to upset Issy, but she doesn't do so well at seeing anything from anyone else's standpoint. What's best for her will be best for Issy. That said," he broke off, "there might have been a hint of an apology when we spoke. I don't know how you did it, Kate, whatever you said, but thank you. Because of you, I have Issy. What you've done for me . . . and after the way I treated you . . . You're amazing."

"You were upset. If anyone tried to take Charlie away from me, I'd probably go completely nuts."

"Still, you went above and beyond."

"I guess I must love you too," she said, locking her eyes with Joe's.

"Not half as much as I love you," he said, tentatively moving towards her.

Kate couldn't seem to stop her body from responding to his and she mirrored his advance . . .

Until her brain snapped back into action; this declaration, oh so wonderful as it was, didn't actually solve any of the problems she and Joe faced if they wanted to try for a future together. Problems that seemed even bigger now she'd had a taste of the downside of celebrity life. They loved one another, but how could this be enough?

"What are we going to do, Joe?" she asked sadly, stepping back. "You'll be returning to America soon, and I can't come with you."

"That's the thing though! With Issy staying here, there's no need for me for go anywhere. And Genevieve's talking about buying a house in the UK; she's planning to bid against the Beckhams for some Gothic pile apparently."

"But . . . what about your work? There's not a lot of call for rock stars in Devon I'm afraid. You need to be based in LA or London at least."

"I've had my time travelling around the world, I don't want that anymore."

"But you've been writing new music, you've been so pleased! You can't let your songs not be heard, it would be such a waste."

"They'll be heard; it just won't be me singing them. I've spoken to my record company and told them I'm not interested in being in the limelight anymore," he said firmly. "I'm done with all that."

"Performing's what you love — it's what you do!" Kate insisted.

"No!" He shook his head. "It's never been about the performing. You know me, I've never actually been all that confident on stage, I just try to cover that up as well as I can. Creating music — writing songs — is the important part for me, that's what I want to do. But I could live without that if I had to. What I love, and what I can't do without, is you."

Kate held her breath, not quite believing it. "Are you sure you'd be happy to walk away from the glitz and the glamour?"

"I'll have absolutely no problem leaving all that rubbish behind."

"So . . . we can be together?" Kate asked tentatively.

"If you want us to be," replied Joe. "It won't be completely plain sailing. I doubt the press will be happy to just leave us alone, and of course our priority must be protecting the children from them and anyone who'd want to harm us because of who I am: I'm afraid you'll have to get used to having the bodyguards around."

"I think I can cope with that," said Kate, smiling.

"It will be difficult to live here," Joe explained. "The press know about it, and my security team have been over the grounds and say it definitely won't be easy for them to work here. There's the fact that it's just so open and then there's the guests coming and going . . ."

"So we'll live somewhere else," said Kate immediately. "I can sell up, or better still Nick could run the business for me. He knows it well and hates his job!"

"Do you think he'd be interested?"

"I can't guarantee it, but I really think so. Though I don't know what I'd then do for work."

"You don't need to do anything Kate; I've got more than enough money to support us."

"I'm not just going to sit around spending your money, Joe."

"Alright, start your own business then, doing whatever you want."

"Well, I did that once. I suppose I could do it again!" She grinned.

"And you're certain you really wouldn't mind giving up your home?"

She didn't need to think about that "problem". Despite her time and, literally, her blood, sweat and tears invested in the place, she knew her answer: "Home is where the people you love are, it's not a place or a building." She touched Joe's hand lightly. "Anyway, somehow I don't think we'd get all your music equipment into my little farmhouse. And don't you need some sort of special soundproofed studio room?"

"Yes, a studio will be very important, especially if we're going to stay in Devon. I want to be able to work from home as much as possible and not have to be rushing back and forth to London all the time to use one."

"I'd like to stay nearby if we can, to be near my mum."

"That's not a problem. Umm . . . so I've actually got a confession to make."

Kate raised an eyebrow.

"Don't get mad, I can explain. I kind of already own a house near here." She stared at him as he continued, "The one we visited the day we went sailing together."

"The huge white house on the coast your friend owns?"

"It's not owned by a friend . . .The house is mine, I bought it years ago. It's where my driver was staying while I was here."

"What? Well, why didn't you just go there when you and Genevieve broke up? It looked like the perfect place to escape to and get over a bad break up."

"That's where I was headed. I needed time away from everything to work out what I wanted to do; not about Genevieve — that had been over for a long time — but for me, and my career. I'd flown into Heathrow and was in London for the night. I was alone, feeling a bit nostalgic being back in the country, back in London. I was thinking of the past, of how things all started. And I was thinking of you. I'd had quite the crush on you at school you know." He smiled. "I was far too shy to say anything, but I was seriously smitten. Then you called and left me that message. I heard your voice again. I looked you up online, saw you had the barns — I couldn't believe we'd actually ended up in the same part of Devon. It's a small world. I had to come, to see you. And, to be honest, I didn't want to be by myself — lonely in my great big house. So I hid the truth. When I was with you again things just felt . . . like the old days between us. I didn't want to mention the house

179

then in case you wanted me to leave, because of the secrecy and all — I didn't want to spoil it. And after I took you sailing there, I didn't know how to come clean! I'd dug a bit of a hole for myself. I know I made your life difficult, but I was loving every minute I spent with you and Charlie, I was falling in love with you. And I was finally — *finally* — writing songs again . . . I didn't think it would blow up the way it did. I knew there were risks, but I would never want to hurt you or Charlie. I got so cross and worked up in part I think because deep down I blamed myself so much. I . . . I love you, Kate." He stopped, out of words, and waited for judgement.

"You're an idiot Joseph Wild." She looked at him hard. "But you're my idiot. You should have told me it was your house."

"Yes, I should," admitted Joe.

"I guess I understand. And I am glad that you're writing again. You've been going through a pretty rough time and it's understandable you had trouble creating music. And when things started to settle down, it came back to you — you're a very talented musician."

"It was more than that. It wasn't being relaxed that helped me, inspired me again. It was you."

Despite herself, Kate blushed. "Well, prepare to keep being inspired. I'm afraid you're stuck with me Joe, for as long as you want me."

"That suits me just fine," he replied, kissing her softly on the lips.

They broke apart and involuntarily, Kate let out a huge yawn, "I'm so sorry! It's been a really long day."

"You've started me off now," said Joe, laughing as he attempted to stifle a yawn of his own.

"Why don't we go to bed?" suggested Kate. "There's plenty of time to talk tomorrow."

"Now that," he grinned, "is a very good idea."

And Kate's rock star took her hand, and led her upstairs, ready to begin their very un-rock'n'roll life together.

THE END

Thank you for reading this book.

If you enjoyed it please leave feedback on Amazon or Goodreads, and if there is anything we missed or you have a question about, then please get in touch. We appreciate you choosing our book.

Founded in 2014 in Shoreditch, London, we at Joffe Books pride ourselves on our history of innovative publishing. We were thrilled to be shortlisted for Independent Publisher of the Year at the British Book Awards.

www.joffebooks.com

We're very grateful to eagle-eyed readers who take the time to contact us. Please send any errors you find to corrections@joffebooks.com. We'll get them fixed ASAP.

Lightning Source UK Ltd.
Milton Keynes UK
UKHW011430181222
414118UK00002B/31